DUCK'S SALVATION

SATAN'S LEGACY MC

ANDI RHODES

BLUE JOURNEY PUBLISHING

Also by Andi Rhodes

Satan's Legacy MC

Snow's Angel

Toga's Demons

Magic's Torment

Duck's Salvation

Dip's Flame

Devil's Handmaidens MC

Harlow's Gamble

For Darcie - Without you, the twists and turns in this book would not be as twisty and turny.

A NOTE FROM THE AUTHOR:

For those of you who read my books, you know I don't always do trigger warnings or a heads up on difficult topics. But I am with Duck's Salvation. This book contains potentially triggering instances relating to miscarriage and other related topics. Please feel free to reach out me at andirhodes@andirhodes.com if you would like more detailed information.

SATAN'S LEGACY MC

DENVER, CO CHAPTER

What the patch binds together,
let no force tear apart.
Satan's Legacy now and forever.

PROLOGUE

DUCK

Six months ago...

"Do you have to go?"

I shove my legs into my jeans and pull the denim up over my hips. Heather, on the other hand, stretches out on the bed, with her hair splayed over the pillow, and her engagement ring winks at me in the minimal light.

"You know I've got club business to deal with today," I remind her.

We've been together for a while now, having met at the homeless shelter she works at, the same one Satan's Legacy MC provides security for. It took a while for me to ask her out, but after my brothers started dropping like flies into the relationship pool, I realized I wanted what they had. Heather and I have been together ever since.

I reach into my dresser to pull out a T-shirt and put it on before grabbing my cut from the hook by the door and slip-

1

ping my arms into it. Sliding my cell into the inside pocket, my fingertips brush over something else. I pull it out and freeze.

My gaze darts to Heather, who's grinning like the Cheshire Cat, and back to the little pink and white stick gripped in my hand.

"Seriously?" I ask, my voice cracking a bit.

Heather nods, but when I remain where I'm standing, her face falls.

"You're not happy."

I stare at the two pink lines for a moment, trying to decipher the emotions rolling through me. Am I happy? I take a deep breath. Fuck yes, I'm happy.

I close the distance between us and climb up the bed to hover above her. "I'm beyond happy, Heather," I tell her, sincerity bleeding into my words. "Way beyond happy."

My lips press against hers and her body immediately arches into mine, seeking more contact. I swallow her groans as my hand travels down her cheek, over her collar-bone, and farther still to rest over her still-flat stomach.

"How far along are you?" I ask against her lips.

Heather shrugs, and the corner of her mouth tips up. "Just took the test yesterday. Still need to schedule a doctor's appointment to confirm."

I rest my forehead against hers. "I love you, Heather."

"I love you, too."

Spreading my palm over her stomach, I glance in that direction. "And I'm going to love this little bean so much."

"I know, Duck." Heather throws her arms around my neck. "I'm so fucking excited. I know we wanted to wait until after we were married, but I'm not upset it didn't work out that way."

"It's working out per—"

"Church, now!"

Snow's shout, accompanied by his thumping on the door, has me practically growling. If he weren't my best friend and my president, I'd yank open the door and tell him to fuck off. Unfortunately, that's not how we work, how the club works.

"I'll see ya later," I tell Heather as I back up toward the door.

"Okay. Be careful." Those two words are like armor for me. Anytime I leave Heather to attend to club business, she reminds me to be careful, reminds me that I have someone to come home to and live for.

Two someones.

By the time I stroll into the meeting room, everyone else is already seated around the table. Snow glares at me and when I grin, his scowl deepens. Too damn bad. Nothing can break my good mood.

"Wipe the grin off your face," Dip, our Road Captain spits out. "Just because you're regularly getting laid, doesn't mean you have to rub it in."

"Aw, nobody wanted your ass last night?" I taunt him.

"Jesus, you're disgusting," he snaps.

"Not too disgusting to knock my fiancée up," I quip.

I immediately want to call the words back. For one thing, I have no clue if Heather is even ready to share this bit of information with anyone. And second, the dejected look on Toga's face has me wondering if I somehow pissed him off. I shrug it off. I'm allowed to be thrilled and share it with those I consider family.

"Congrats, bro," Snow says, a genuineness in his tone. "Now, sit down so we can get started."

I move to my seat and sit, knowing there will be time

enough later to celebrate. Church is for club business and demands us to be serious... for the most part.

"What the patch binds together, let no force tear apart. Satan's Legacy now and forever."

After we recite the motto in unison, Snow dives in.

"We're starting to see a spike in a new drug that's making its way through our streets," he begins. "It popped up about two weeks ago. Didn't really think anything of it. Every dealer in the area knows this is Satan's Legacy territory and if that doesn't stop them, we deliver a message. Usually, that's enough."

"It would be enough if we could track this fucker down," Toga snips. "As it stands, all we have is the stupid logo on the pills." He tosses a small plastic baggie onto the table. "A fucking bat... that's all we have to go on. No one knows anything and if they do, they're not talking."

"Ah, that's not true," Magic, our Enforcer, states. "I was able to track down a name."

"And..."

"Dracula."

"Seriously?" I ask, throwing my head back and laughing. "That's the best the punk could come up with? Dracula?"

"I couldn't give two shits less what the leader's name is," Snow snaps. "How do we find him and shut him down?"

"Prez, it's gonna take time," Toga says. "This guy, or bitch, is a ghost. No one knows what they look like, where they're operating out of... nothing."

Snow pounds his fist into the table, rattling the coffee mugs scattered on top. "We need to figure this out! I don't like competition, but more than that, I don't like drugs that are an unknown. There's already been one overdose attributed to these pills, and I have a feeling it's going to get a lot worse."

"We have these," Toga says as he lifts the baggie he tossed down earlier. "Can we get it tested, see what we're working with?"

"Yeah. And we will." Snow heaves a sigh. "I don't like this. Not one bit."

"None of us do, Prez," I say. "But it's the situation we have, so we handle it. We'll find them and take them out."

Snow runs a hand through his hair. "Yeah, I know we will. But I'd rather it be before it permeates the shelters we're tied to. This is one shit show we don't have our hand in, and I'd like to keep it that way." He rises from his chair. "Any other business before I call it?"

"Nah, brother," Magic says. "I'll reach out to a contact I have who can figure out what the pills are made of. Once we have that, we'll have a better direction to go in."

"Good, get it done," Snow barks. "Now get the fuck out of here."

As the others file out of the room, I stay behind to talk to Snow.

"What's up, man? You're unusually wound up about this."

Snow lifts his gaze to mine. "I don't know, Duck. I just..."

"Have a feeling," I finish for him.

He nods. "This shit isn't going to end quickly or easily. It's gonna be way too late for a lot of people."

"Anything specific giving you this feeling?"

"No. That's what fucking sucks. I can't explain it. I just know."

"Your gut is rarely, if ever, wrong. Trust it."

"I am. But what the fuck does it matter when we have nothing?"

"It matters."

Snow chuckles. "Yeah. Okay." Then he grins at me. "So, gonna be a daddy, huh?"

I return his expression ten-fold. "Seems like it."

"And you're good with this?"

"I'm good. I'm thrilled."

"Then I'm happy for you."

"Thanks, bro."

As we walk out of the room, my heart is full. My soul is calm for the first time. Despite all this Dracula bullshit, I'm on an emotional high that can't be destroyed.

I should've known that, in my world, the happier you are, the harder you fucking fall.

CHAPTER I

GRACE

PRESENT DAY...

"Time of death..."

I tune out the rest of the doctor's words, having heard them many times over. The only thing that ever changes is the time itself and the lifeless patient lying on the bed. Today is shaping up to be another in a long line of days filled with preventable deaths. This is the second overdose since my shift started three hours ago.

Removing my gloves with a snap of the latex, I move to the deceased's belongings and dig in his pockets for identification. His family will need to be notified. Thank God I'm not the one responsible for those sorts of notifications. I don't think I could handle it.

When my fingers wrap around a plastic baggie in the front pocket of the guy's jeans, I heave a sigh because I know what I'm going to see when I pull it out. It's the same thing I've seen on at least fifteen of the other overdose deaths in the last few months.

"Again?" the doctor asks, nodding at the baggie full of red pills with a black bat imprinted on them.

"Seems like." I set the drugs aside and continue looking

for identification. I latch on to what feels like a wallet and pull it out to open it. "Dammit," I grumble when I look at the license.

"What?"

"He's only sixteen." I flip the plastic card around to show it to the doctor. "He's only had this for a month. He's just a stupid kid."

"Unfortunately, Grace, drugs don't discriminate."

With a look of disgust, he shakes his head and walks out the door. For him, this is over. The patient died and the doctor has to move on, putting any actual emotion out of his mind. At least for the remainder of his shift.

I spare a glance for the sixteen-year-old who went left when he should have gone right before stepping into the hallway. The emergency department is crowded, but that's normal for a level one trauma center. We see it all, treat it all, but don't always win them all. It's part of the job, the only part I hate.

"We'll drink one for him tonight, chicky."

Turning to Vince, another nurse and one of my best friends, I force a smile and bump my shoulder into his.

"Thanks."

Vince shrugs. "It's tradition," he says before rushing to respond to a doctor shouting his name.

He's right, it's tradition. For every death that happens on our shifts, we drink. Between me, Vince, and Lucy, another nurse and the third to our BFF trio, we do a lot of drinking. But it never quite silences the always present sadness for those we couldn't save.

"Grace, we've got another!"

Snapping out of my thoughts, I rush to the gurney that's being wheeled in by a paramedic. The same doctor from my last patient is right there with me and we exchange a look, I know another drink will be necessary.

By the time my shift is over, the drink tally is up to seven. It hasn't been that high in a while and I inwardly groan knowing that I'll be dealing with work *and* a hangover tomorrow. After showering and putting on a pair of soft black leggings and a green hoodie, I call for an Uber and wait in front of the hospital for it to arrive.

"There you are," Lucy says when she spots me walking through the door of the local pub that we've made our hangout spot. She races toward me and slips her arm around my shoulders to steer me toward the table she and Vince have secured. "I thought you'd be here an hour ago."

"Me too," I say ruefully. "Motor vehicle accident came in at the last minute." Lucy arches a brow at me. "No, that patient is not on our list tonight. He's gonna be sporting some hardware, but he'll be fine."

"So, what's the number?" Vince asks when we sit down.

"Seven."

Vince whistles. "Shit, that's a lot."

Lucy reaches for my hand and squeezes it. "Why is it death always seems to find you?"

I wince at her words, recalling one particular death that will never leave me, no matter how many drinks I consume.

"I take it neither of you have any to add to that total."

Lucy shakes her head. "Thought I would but was able to bring him back with the paddles."

"I've got one," Vince tells us. "Overdose."

"Jesus," I mumble, scrubbing my hands over my face. "That seems to be the majority of what we see anymore, ever since those new pills hit the streets. What the fuck are they?"

"No one knows. I've been questioned by police so many

times," Lucy tells us. "They're grasping at straws and trying to latch onto anything that might point them in the right direction. Unfortunately, I never have any new information for them. There's no common denominator with the patients that I can see, and each death is different."

"Same here," Vince says. "All I know is they're over-doses. And the only reason we even know they're connected somehow is because we find the evidence when looking through the belongings for identification. It's crazy."

I wave my hand in an effort to dismiss the conversation. I don't want to talk about the people we lost today or the stupid red pills. I just want to drink in their honor and let the alcohol numb me.

Forcing a smile, I focus my attention on Vince. "So, my friend, how'd the date go last night?"

He rolls his eyes as he leans back in his chair. Before he can answer, Lucy rises to her feet and says, "I'm gonna go grab us a pitcher and some shots." She shoots daggers at Vince. "Save the good stuff for when I get back."

Once she's gone, Vince leans forward again. "Grace, seriously, are you okay?"

Vince is my best friend, the first friend I made after moving to Denver. I was a traveling nurse at the time and so tired of running from the nightmares that plagued me regardless of geography. On my first on-call shift, I decided to catch some sleep in the break room and was startled awake by a flamboyant and cocky nurse who was shaking me in an effort to wake me.

There was something in his eyes that told me to trust him, to share my burdens with him because he'd be able to bring some color into my pitch-black existence. That was four years ago and even though the darkness hovers at the edges, Vince always adds that pop of sparkly color that I need to keep me sane.

"I'm good, Vince. Promise."

He eyes me skeptically, his expression telling me he's going to question me further, but just then Lucy is back, and the spell is broken. Vince knows my secrets, every last one. Lucy doesn't. Not because I don't trust her but because Lucy tends to always find the bright side of things and I can't do that, not with this.

"Okay, big guy, spill it," Lucy prompts, an excited and expectant look on her face. "Let us live vicariously through your wicked ways."

"Honey, last night was particularly wicked." Vince winks. "Sure you can handle it?"

Lucy squeals with delight. "Bring it."

And bring it he does. Vince goes on for the next hour about his most recent boy toy and all the *fun* he had last night. Lucy hangs on to every single word while I hear only about fifty percent of his sordid tales.

Two pitchers of beer and a total of twenty-one shots later, the three of us stumble outside to wait for our respective Ubers. Lucy and Vince share one as they are heading in the same direction. When mine arrives, I climb in and rest my head against the seat, my eyes sliding closed.

Today was a long day. Shit, the last five years have been the longest of my life. And I don't know if it's the alcohol swirling in my system or a genuine gut feeling, but something tells me that I'm in for many more long days full of pain and haunting memories.

CHAPTER 2
DUCK
THREE WEEKS LATER...

"I wish you were with me."

I absently tap my fingers against the table in the meeting room. I have Heather's call on speakerphone while I wait for the others to get here for church. Normally, I'd be driving Heather to the OB-GYN, but not today. No, I'm needed here, which takes precedence over a routine check-up.

I picture Heather rubbing her growing belly protectively. So far, the pregnancy has been great. Sure she went through morning sickness and all the normal shit women have to deal with, but she's handled it like a champ.

I, on the other hand, have not. So any chance I get to hear my little girl's heartbeat and see her on that black and white grainy monitor, I take it. I live for those appointments.

But Snow called church, and I'm stuck here while Little Man, a prospect for the club, is following behind Heather to make sure she arrives at the doctor's office safe and sound. All because of stupid red pills and a fucker who calls himself Dracula.

It's been months and we're still no closer to tracking down this guy, and the pills keep on coming, as well as the deaths. We've had four people now in the shelter Heather works at pass away due to overdosing on the shit.

We thought we'd catch a break when we got our hands on the chemical breakdown of the drug, but no such luck. We keep running into dead end after dead end. Dracula is a ghost, despite the very real presence of his work.

"You know I'd be there if I could, but I've got—"

"Yeah, yeah," she huffs. "Club business."

It's always club business, and Heather is great about it, knowing there will never be a time when I can tell her everything. But that doesn't mean either of us has to like it. She's going to be my ol' lady, the mother of my child, and it fucking sucks keeping things from her.

"So, did you get a chance to look at the list I sent you?" I ask her in an effort to steer the conversation to other things.

Heather snorts. "You mean that list that you think was of baby names?"

I grin. "Hey, they were baby names."

"C'mon, asshole," Heather mutters. "Not you, Duck. Just some idiot who doesn't know how to share the road. Anyway, no, those weren't baby names. I mean, Helga? Really?"

"So you prefer Vaginay?" I tease, soaking up her giggle.

"You're ridiculous, you know that, right?"

"Yeah, but you're smiling now."

"I am."

And she is. I can hear it in her voice. The baby name conversation always puts her in a good mood. The only problem is, we can't agree on any one name.

"How about Selma?"

The door to the meeting room opens slowly as my brothers begin to file into the room.

"Definitely not Selma," I tell her.

"If you both would listen to me, you wouldn't still be trying to figure this shit out," Snow grumbles when he sits down next to me.

"We're not naming our little girl Zekette," Heather groans.

"Definitely not," I agree.

"You say that now," Snow begins with a grin on his face as he leans in close to my cell. "But once you see—"

Shattering glass, the squeal of tires, and Heather's screams are deafening coming through the line, and my body tenses with fear and panic. My brothers crowd around me, worried expressions on all their faces.

"Heather?" I shout into the phone. "Heather, what happened?"

Nothing.

"Heather!"

I'm dimly aware of Snow issuing orders to the others, but my focus remains on whatever is happening that I can't see. Sirens begin to filter in through my foggy brain, mixing with the thudding footsteps of those running around me and my racing heart.

A shuffling sound comes through the line.

"Heather?" I ask, praying it's her moving around. "Heather, can you hear me?"

"Duck, it's Little Man," the voice on the other end replies. "You need to get to the hospital now. I'll follow the ambulance."

"Is she okay?" I ask as I rush around the table and through the clubhouse toward my bike, Snow hot on my heels.

"I..." Little Man clears his throat. "I don't know, D. It's bad."

"What the fuck happened?" I demand, throwing a leg over my Harley and firing her up.

My phone is yanked from my hand by Snow, and he steps out of my reach when I try to get it back.

"Little Man, stay with her. You can fill us in at the hospital," my president orders before disconnecting the call and stepping close to stuff my cell in my cut pocket. "We're taking the truck."

"Fuck that!"

"Duck, get off the bike. You're in no condition to drive. Now," he growls.

I do as ordered, my brain spinning a mile a minute. Two minutes later, Snow is stomping on the gas and taking me to my girls.

Please God, let them be okay.

I repeat this plea over and over again the entire way to the hospital. I have no idea if there even is a God, or if he or she would entertain the notion of helping a man who has a space reserved in Hell, but I have to do something.

Twenty minutes later, I'm barreling through the doors of the emergency department only to be met with an arm wrapping around my waist to slow me down. I glare down at the offending arm and then up to the face of the man it belongs to.

"Little Man," I growl in warning. "Where is she?"

Snow grabs me from behind and holds me in place so Little Man can let go. "Answer him, prospect," he demands. "Where's Heather?"

Little Man's face falls. "In surgery."

Every ounce of strength I have dissipates under those

two words. Heather can't be in surgery. She's pregnant. So many things can go wrong.

Snow and Little Man each take an arm and lead me toward the elevators.

"They wouldn't tell me anything because I'm not family, but a nurse did tell me where we could wait until Heather is out of surgery."

I nod at Little Man absentmindedly. I focus on putting one foot in front of the other until I'm pushed into a chair in what I assume is the surgical waiting room. Satan's Legacy brothers trickle in and begin to fill up the seats around me until the room becomes crowded and smells of fear, anger, and motor oil.

Some try to talk to me while others give me a wide berth, none of it brings me from the numb void threatening to swallow me whole.

"Mason Howard?"

I whip my head up at my given name, but after seeing the exhausted expression on the doctor's face, I can't make my body follow my command to stand and move.

"He's right here," Snow says from his position next to me.

The doctor walks toward me, and my stomach cramps at the sight of blood covering his light green scrubs. So much fucking blood.

"Mr. Howard, are you Heather Smith's fiancé?"

I nod, unable to form any words.

The doctor blows out a breath and his lips tip up at the corners. I want to reach out and snap his neck because there is nothing to smile about right now, but his words shut down my murderous thoughts.

"Ms. Smith is currently in a recovery room and should be fine once the anesthesia wears off." His lips fall and he clears his throat. "Unfortunately, we had to perform an emergency C-section due to a placental rupture caused by the seat belt during the accident. She lost a lot of blood, but she's a fighter."

"But she's only seven months pregnant," I snap, slowly coming out of my haze. He hasn't said the baby is dead and Heather is okay, so maybe it's not as bad as it sounds. "That's too early, right? I mean, she's not due for another..."

My words trail off when the doctor holds up his hand. "You're right, it's early. But your daughter is alive and in the NICU. Her lungs are underdeveloped, but they're working, which is great. The first few days will be critical, but I'm confident that, with the appropriate care, she'll be just fine. For now, we just need to give it time and let her doctors do what they do best."

"When can I see her?"

"Once the pediatrician is done with her assessments, she'll come get you and take you to see your daughter."

"Yeah, okay, but..." I shove a shaky hand through my hair. "When can I see Heather?"

"Let's give her a little time, and I'll have a nurse let you know when it's okay for her to have visitors."

Again, I nod. The doctor disappears through a set of double doors, and Snow throws his arms around my shoulders.

"Congrats Dad."

"Huh?"

He shakes me. "You've got a little girl, man." My best friend is grinning at me, no doubt holding onto the positive words that came out of the doctor's mouth, but all I can hear is Heather's screams, the sound of terror that will forever haunt my subconscious, reminding me that I wasn't there to protect her.

"We're gonna go get some coffee." I lift my head and see Toga and Magic standing in front of me. "Want anything?" Toga asks.

I shake my head as Snow says, "Bring us both a coffee and add a shot of whiskey to Duck's."

"Uh, Prez, we're in a hospital," Magic reminds him. "Don't think we'll be able to find any alcohol in this joint."

"Make it happen," Snow snaps.

"On it," Toga quips as he practically drags Magic away.

No one says another word as we sit here, although I can feel the stares of every man and woman in the room. At some point, a cup is thrust into my hand, and I'm grateful when I take a sip and the burn of whiskey travels through my body.

As I stare at the floor, and long after my legs fall asleep and my ass is numb from the uncomfortable plastic chair, a pair of sneaker clad feet enter my line of sight. I slowly lift my head, bracing myself for bad news.

"Mr. Howard?"

"Yeah, that's, um..." I swallow. "That's me."

"If you'll follow me, I can take you to see Heather."

When I stand, I have to shake my legs to get the blood flowing again. A thousand pinpricks dance along my limbs, but I ignore them as I follow the middle-aged nurse. I glance over my shoulder to see Snow still sitting, his watchful stare encouraging me to keep putting one foot in front of the other.

It feels like hours pass before we reach a room on the fifth floor. The nurse stops at room five sixteen and turns to face me.

"She's still a little groggy, so please keep the visit brief."

"And my daughter?" I prod. I haven't been able to go see her, even though I was told I could. But I know Heather will be asking about her, and I don't have any news at this point to share except that she's alive.

"I'll have her brought up so you can both see her together." Her kind smile falters for a split second, but she recovers quickly. "You won't be able to hold her, as she's in an incubator, but you'll be able to see her, talk to her, and touch her through the arm holes."

I nod and the nurse steps to the side so I can open the door to Heather's room. The wooden barrier creaks slightly on its hinges, but it swings open effortlessly. The room is bathed in fluorescent light and when my gaze falls on the bed, my recently relaxing muscles tense to an impossible degree because the bed is empty.

And on the rolling table that is a fixture of every hospital room is the ring I slipped on Heather's finger months ago when she said 'yes' and a note.

CHAPTER 3
GRACE

I flinch as the man in room five sixteen, the one with a horned skull patch on his leather vest, throws the bedside table at the wall, causing it to splinter apart and crash onto the floor. My hands flatten in a protective manner against the plastic of the incubator, as if I can protect the little peanut inside from the chaos her father is creating.

Several security guards rush past me, but they're barely a blip on my radar as I focus on the destruction they're running toward.

"Poor thing."

I turn to my right and am surprised to see Vince taking in the scene with a shake of his head.

"Which one?" I ask. "The baby or him?" I nod toward the room.

"Both." Vince shrugs. "Do you know what happened?"

"No. I was asked to bring the daughter so her parents could see her, but by the time I got here, he was already destroying everything." I narrow my eyes at him. "Why are you up here anyway? Aren't you supposed to be down in the ER?"

"Same as you, chicky. The ER is slow, and they sent me up here. Looks like we'll still be working our shift together."

I roll my eyes. We're always working the same shifts. Not that I'm complaining. But I don't believe for one second that Vince was sent up here to help. It's more likely that he requested to be moved to this post after I was assigned up here because he knew I'd be dealing with babies. And babies are hard for me.

I look down at the little pink bundle, a shiver racing up my spine when the memory of another flash of pink assaults my mind.

I squeeze my daughter to my chest, silent tears streaming down my face as Carter spews his venom at me.

"You're worthless," he seethes, his chest rising and falling with his panting breaths. "Absolutely worthless."

I don't bother defending his accusation, the evidence cradled in my arms. After eleven grueling hours, our daughter was still-born, the umbilical cord having been wrapped around her neck for too long. Carter, my fiancé, blames me because I'm a nurse. He thinks I should have somehow known.

And maybe he's right. I should've known something was wrong. The doctors and nurses who provided my prenatal care should've known. Only that's not true. Sometimes things happen, awful things that are beyond our control.

Glass shattering pulls my attention from our daughter in time to see a broken vase full of daisies falling to the floor. I look at Carter out of the corner of my eye, watching him warily as he paces the room, no doubt in search of something else to break. I've never seen him like this, so totally out of control and enraged. He's always been sweet to me. Hell, I'm going to marry him.

"Where's the doctor?" he fumes at me. "Why can't they take that, that... "He points to the pink mass in my arms. "... thing from the room?"

My heart skips a beat or five at his callous description of our little girl and I snap.

"Thing?" I ask quietly as I sit up a little straighter, ignoring the total physical and mental exhaustion I'd give anything to succumb to. "Thing?" I enunciate, louder this time. "This thing is your daughter!"

Carter stops next to my bed and glares down at me. I want to reach out and smack the sanctimonious look off his face, but I refuse to let go of my baby.

"She's dead, Grace," he deadpans, anger still threaded in his tone. "Dead and as worthless as her mother."

I feel the blood drain from my face as his words suck the life out of me just as effectively as a Hoover sucks up dust. My shoulders deflate and air rushes past my lips as I exhale.

"I've wasted four years on you," Carter says with as much enthusiasm as one would have reading a grocery list. "Four years, Grace. And for what? The one thing you should be able to give me, you can't. You're defective, a disgusting piece of—"

"Grace!"

I shake my head as vigorously as the hands shaking my shoulders.

"I'm sorry," I whisper brokenly.

Vince pulls me to his chest and wraps his arms around me. I cry against him, letting him absorb the pain my memories force upon me.

"Shh, chicky. You've got nothing to be sorry for."

"Br-broken."

Vince doesn't say another word, fully aware that it doesn't matter what he says, or anyone else for that matter.

Carter's voice will forever remain in my head, always fighting for dominance over sanity, over positivity.

Several minutes pass before I extricate myself from Vince's arms and shuffle backward a few steps. I glance around my surroundings and take in the dark, empty room. Vince sees the questions that are no doubt dancing in my eyes and explains.

"I pulled you in here as soon as I realized what was happening. Another nurse returned the baby to the NICU."

Numbly, I nod.

"Why don't you go take a break, pull yourself together?"

I swipe at the wetness still clinging to my cheeks and take a deep breath. "I'm okay. Um, how long was I out of it?"

"Not long. Five minutes maybe."

"Five minutes too long," I mumble. At Vince's stern look, I glance toward the hallway. "Did he ever calm down?"

"Who?"

"The father."

Vince chuckles, but there's no humor in it. "Nope. Security hasn't even been able to get near him. The room is completely destroyed." He sighs, and if I'm not mistaken, there's a little dreamy quality to it. "Why can't I find a man like that?"

"Like what?" I huff out. "Intimidating, scary, dangerous?"

"That's gonna be your downfall someday, Grace. You only see the destruction, but I see the utter helplessness of a man in love." He grins. "And where you see strength used to inflict harm, I see muscle designed to dominate and own me in the bedroom."

A snort escapes me, and I slap him on the arm. "Do you ever think about anything other than sex?"

"Did you not hear the part where I mentioned love?"

"Yeah, yeah."

Knowing that Vince's teasing has temporarily released me from my mental hell, I force my feet to carry me to the door and my hand to grip the knob and pull it open. Time to get back to reality. As soon as I step into the hallway, movement catches my eye and I swing my head to the right.

Four security guards are standing at the door of room five sixteen, animatedly talking, but I can't hear their words. The sound of furniture and items being decimated isn't filling the air, but the shouts and rages coming from inside the room are.

My heart cracks at the man's torment. I don't know what happened, what triggered his outburst, but a part of me suddenly needs to find out. I couldn't fix my broken pieces, but maybe I can find a way to help him fix his... or at least be there to help keep them contained so he can try to fit them back together at a later date.

This is it, Grace. You've lost your damn mind.

"Shit, I know that look," Vince says as he steps out of the room to stand next to me.

"What look?"

"That I'm-gonna-bury-my-pain-and-give-in-to-some-one-else's look."

"I don't do that," I insist.

"Yeah, you do," he counters. "You hide behind other's problems so you don't have to face your own. It's part of what makes you a damn good nurse. You always put everyone else above yourself. But Grace, you can't save everyone. Not every person is salvageable."

I stiffen at his words because that's exactly what I

thought people saw when they looked at me after losing my baby and my fiancé all in the space of a few hours. That I wasn't salvageable. But look at me now. I'm better. I was salvaged from the wreckage of my life.

If that's what helps you sleep at night.

I take off running down the hall, toward the elevators, an idea forming in my mind. Ignoring Vince's hollers for me to stop, I slip between the doors as soon as they slide open and stab my finger on the button for the floor I need to get to.

When they open again, I stride toward the waiting area where I'm met with a sea of denim and leather. Men, women, and a few children have taken over the relatively small space. Some are sleeping, others are engaged in hushed conversations, and a few are awake and alert, their eyes constantly scanning the room.

My presence is instantly known, and several sets of eyes settle on me. I know exactly who these people are, who the man on the fifth floor is. You can't live in this area and not at least know about the Satan's Legacy MC. But I have to admit, they aren't as intimidating as the stories made me believe.

I scan the leather until I find the one with a patch that reads 'President' and make my way toward him. After I take a few steps, he stands and comes at me, a hard glint in his eye that should alarm me. But it doesn't, because I recognize it for what it truly is... worry.

"I take it you're all the family of Heather Smith and her baby?" I say, more confidence in my voice than I thought there'd be.

The man narrows his gaze, as if surprised. "We are. I'm Snow." He sticks out his hand and I shake it. "Is everything okay? Duck... I mean Mason is up with Heather now, so whatever news you have nee—"

"You need to come with me," I tell him.

I turn back around and walk toward the elevators, heavy footsteps following in my wake. Before I get too far, I look over my shoulder at Snow.

"You might want to bring a few of your guys with you." I smile sadly and nod to the others remaining behind.

"Why's that?" he asks me skeptically.

"Because this particular battle is going to be like nothing you've ever seen."

CHAPTER 4

DUCK

on't look for me because you won't like what you find.

... you won't like what you find.

A red haze lingers, hovering over my vision, tinging everything I see with a deep and unforgiving rage as the only sentence in the note replays in my brain, over and over again. I swivel my head back and forth, seeking out something else I can destroy. The room is a mess, and not much remains untouched. The television that had been mounted on the wall is in pieces on the floor, along with numerous other items my hands got a hold of.

I don't know how long I've been on my rampage. My muscles aren't screaming at me yet, so not long enough. I want to continue unleashing my wrath outside this room, but I know if the four security guards just outside the door touch me in an effort to halt my destruction, I'll kill 'em.

Pulling my knife from my boot, I stab it through the bedding and into the mattress. I drag it through the material, the tearing sound feeding the beast inside me. All the while, one question keeps playing through my mind: Why?

"Duck!"

Spinning around at my name being shouted, my glare lands on Snow, Toga, Dip, and Magic, all of whom are pounding on the door demanding entry. I ignore them, but a minute later, the wooden barrier splinters beneath a kick by Snow, the small window also breaking.

"Get the fuck out of here," I seethe, holding my knife out in front of me to ward them off.

A part of my brain snaps back to reality and reminds me that they mean me no harm, that they aren't the bad guys in this fucked up situation. But the other parts, the enraged parts, don't give a damn. I need to keep going, keep my fury at the forefront of my thoughts because if I don't, if I stop, I'll break. I'll crumble beneath the agony of finding Heather gone.

"Not happening," Snow snaps. "You need to calm down."

"Calm down?! How the fuck am I supposed to calm down?"

I track Magic and Toga's movements as they shift to either side of the room.

"I don't think so," I grit out as I swing my knife through the air to indicate all of them.

"Duck, brother, what the hell happened?" Dip asks from his position next to Snow with his hands held up in front of him. "Why are you tearing this room a new asshole?"

I shove my hand into my pocket and pull out the engagement ring Heather left behind to hold it up for them to see. All four of them eye the diamond, recognition flaring in their stares. Next, I pull out the crumpled-up piece of paper and throw it to the floor.

Snow takes a step toward me, then another when I don't react. Don't get me wrong, I try to react, but my body isn't cooperating. He bends to pick up the discarded note and viciously swears under his breath when he reads it. When he returns his attention to me, there's pity in his eyes, which only fans the flames of my anger.

Stop! Just leave me alone.

"This..." Snow sweeps his arm to indicate the room. "... isn't the answer."

"This is the only answer!"

"It's not, and you know it," he insists. "You're a father now, D. Is this really the version of you that you want your daughter to see for the first time?"

At the mention of my daughter, my knees buckle. I mentally brace for the impact, but before I hit the floor, Toga and Magic rush forward and hold me up. My rage is replaced by emotions I don't want to identify. Emotions that, for the last twenty minutes or so, I've tried to keep at bay because they make me vulnerable in a way I never remember being before in my life.

"I have no goddamn clue how to be a dad," I push out.

"Who the hell does? I certainly didn't when Zoe was born, even though I'd been a father figure to Shiloh for some time already," Magic blurts. "Kids don't come with a user manual, bro. You do what every other man on the planet does when they have a kid... fake it until you make it."

"He's right," Snow insists. "You'll figure it out as you go. But first you've gotta get yourself under control."

I shake my head. "It wasn't supposed to be like this. I wasn't supposed to be doing this on my own."

Toga snorts, but there's a bitterness to it. "When have you known anything to go the way it's supposed to?"

Before I can answer, Dip adds, "And you're not alone.

Fuck, you've got an entire club by your side, as well as ol' ladies. You're only in this alone if you choose to be."

Each one of them is right, but it's damn hard to hold onto the facts when my blood is still boiling and my head is throbbing with unchecked fury. How could she do this to me? To us?

Does it matter? What's done is done.

I tug out of my brother's hold and start to pace again, but this time my movements aren't punctuated by the need to destroy. No, they're more resigned to the fact that this is now my life. Whatever *this* is.

Swiping the wetness from my cheeks, I ignore the voice in my head that tells me I'm a pussy for letting my emotions get the best of me. I swallow the lump in my throat, forcing it down to settle in my gut like a clump of lead bullets.

I glance around at the damage I caused and inwardly groan at the thought of the price tag the hospital will put on it all. It's definitely not gonna be a cheap fix. But I will fix it. There's no other choice, especially when my little girl's life is in the hands of its doctors.

Speaking of...

"Have any of you seen her yet?" I ask, stopping in front of my brothers.

"Your daughter?" Snow asks. I nod. "No. Have you?"

"No."

"Don't you think you should remedy that?" Toga asks quietly.

I glare at him. "Of course I do, but..."

"But what?"

Heaving a sigh, I run a shaky hand through my hair. "What the fuck do I say to her?"

"Dude, she's not even a day old," Magic snaps. "It's not

like you need to gear up for a political conversation. Hell, it's not even gonna be a conversation. Just... love her."

Love her.

It sounds simple enough, but what if it isn't? What if I look at her and all I see is Heather? What if the part of me that's supposed to be paternal is broken? Or worse yet, missing completely?

Snow grips my shoulder. "I'm gonna go ask one of the nurses to bring her to another patient room so you can see her."

Panic immediately slices through me, and I tense. "But what if—"

"No," Snow commands. "No what ifs. One step at a time, Duck. Okay?"

"Okay."

"Prez, can you, um, take Dip and Magic with you?" Toga asks as he rocks back and forth on the balls of his feet. "I'd like to talk to Duck for a minute."

Snow eyes him suspiciously but after a moment, he nods. "Sure thing."

The three of them shuffle out the door, leaving Toga and me alone.

"What's going on, T?" I ask.

Toga shoves his hands in his pockets as he drops his head back. His cheeks puff up with air and then it whooshes past his lips.

"You need to get your head out of your goddamn ass."

"Excuse me?" I sneer.

He finally looks at me, his eyes locking onto mine in a stare that would have others withering under it.

"I know it's hard right now to see past what Heather did, but you have to."

"I don't have to do anything."

"Yeah, Duck, you do. Because you're not thinking or acting just for yourself anymore." He stabs a finger in the direction of the door. "You've got that little girl to think of now and she's going to need her daddy."

"No shit."

Toga heaves a sigh. "Look, all I'm saying is you have no idea how lucky you are right now. Sure, Heather's gone, but that's not where this story ends. You've got a daughter, Duck. A fucking daughter!"

Does he really think I don't know this?

"What's your point, Toga?"

"My point is..." He averts his gaze for a minute, and I watch as his throat works like he's trying to keep his own emotions in check. When he looks back at me, his face is a mask of sorrow. "My point is, not everyone gets what you've been given."

"And what's that?"

"Jesus, you're not this stupid," he barks. "A kid, Duck. Not everyone gets a kid."

"I feel like you're trying to tell me something while saying a whole lot of nothing," I tell him. "What are you not saying?"

Toga lunges at me, gripping my cut in his hands to pull me close. "I had a chance at what you have," he snarls, his face contorting with pain. "Fallon and me... she was pregnant, Duck. And she miscarried. Our kid died for some unknown reason, and I wouldn't wish that pain on my worst enemy."

My entire body deflates. "I'm sorry, T. I had no idea."

He releases me and shakes his head. "No one did. No one does. I'd like to keep it that way. For Fallon's sake."

"Of course. But why are you telling me?"

"You needed to know." He shrugs. "I can't stand by and

watch you throw away the best thing that's likely to ever happen to you. So, get your shit together and man up. Your daughter is depending on that."

I nod. "I know. And I will."

I hope.

"Good. Because if you don't, VP or not, I'll beat your ass."

Toga starts toward the door, this conversation apparently over.

"Hey, T?"

He glances over his shoulder.

"I'm really sorry for your and Fallon's loss." And I am. As angry as I am at Heather, as pissed off as I am at the circumstances of my situation, the thought of having lost my little girl too is enough to make me go postal. Or more postal.

"Thanks."

"You're not alone either though," I tell him quietly. "You have the same family I do."

"Seems like something we both should remember."

CHAPTER 5
GRACE

I fidget with my hands as I stand outside the trashed patient room. Mason, or Duck as Snow called him, has calmed down considerably, but he's still giving off a dangerous vibe. Don't get me wrong, it's not that I'm getting the sense that he'd hurt me, but more like he has this dark power to bring the world to its knees without a second thought.

My stomach clenches when he stops pacing and stares at me through the open doorway. His brows are drawn down, but his eyes are penetrating. It feels as if he's gazing into my soul and finding me lacking in some way.

Which is unfortunate because my body isn't finding a single inch of anything lacking about him. Physically anyway. I stiffen my spine against the unwanted appreciation coiling through me. This isn't the time or place for a physical reaction to a man. Especially not this man.

After several long moments of staring at one another, I break eye contact. When I look back at him, he's sporting a sardonic grin.

"Are you gonna stand there all day or come tell me what

the fuck you want?" he snarls, looking entirely too aware and pleased that he's getting under my skin.

Get a grip, Grace.

I square my shoulders and stride into the room, coming to a stop several feet away from him.

"I was told you wanted to see your daughter."

"Yet here you are, without her."

I arch a brow, annoyance slithering over me. "And why do you think that is?" I ask with a sweep of my arm.

Duck's face falls for a fraction of a second before he carefully slips his mask of irritation back in place.

"I wouldn't hurt her."

Choosing to ignore that statement, mostly because I believe him and I'm not sure that's wise, I start to turn back toward the door.

"I'll take you to her."

I walk away and don't look back. He's either going to follow me or he's not. That choice is his and his alone.

Heavy footsteps join with my lighter ones just as I'm reaching the elevator. I don't give any outward indication of the relief I experience that he chose to follow. Mason 'Duck' Howard may be an intimidating human being, but something tells me that there's so much more to him than what everyone saw back in that room. No one gets that angry unless there are more complicated emotions driving that anger.

The elevator ride to the NICU floor is silent and tense. Nervous energy rolls off Duck in waves, threatening to consume me in their wake. Out of the corner of my eye, I watch him, study him... memorize him.

No! No, no, no.

When the doors slide open, I step out before Duck can, once again leaving him to follow or not. He falls into step beside me much faster this time. I'm acutely aware of the way his strides slow to match mine, the way his fists clench and unclench at his sides, and the way his body tenses the closer we get to the door of the NICU.

I stop in front of said door and turn to face him.

"Whatever happened in that room downstairs needs to stay there," I tell him. "There are a lot of sick babies and worried families in there." I point to the door. "And they don't need your shit to deal with on top of their own."

Duck's expression hardens as he takes a step toward me. "Listen lady, what happened back there is none of your damn business. And despite what it might look like, I'm not a..." He presses his lips together for a second before continuing. "Ya know what, no. I don't have to explain myself to some nurse with terrible bedside manner. Just take me to see my daughter."

Narrowing my eyes at him, I snap. "I don't see a bedside here so that's not a fair assessment. And I will not apologize for doing what I feel is necessary to protect patients and their families."

"Take me. To see. My daughter."

I turn on my heel and open the door to step through. Immediately, I'm thrown back to another place and time, but I don't even really know why. My daughter didn't make it long enough to be in the NICU. My daughter didn't make it long enough to experience this world at all.

Walking down the aisle to where Duck's daughter is, I nod at the other families and offer them smiles to hopefully brighten their otherwise terrible days here. When we reach the baby we're here to see, Duck gasps and freezes.

"Mr. Howard, meet your daughter."

He takes a tentative step toward the incubator, his eyes scanning the tubes, wires, and machines, looking everywhere but at the pink bundle. Finally, he drops his head and takes in his daughter. The way his eyes soften and his lips turn up slightly at the corners... it's enough to make a woman melt into an ooey-gooey puddle.

But then she wisens up and remembers his little temper tantrum earlier.

Duck flattens his hands over the clear plastic dome. I shift so I can give him some space, but he doesn't let me get far.

"Where are you going?"

"I figured you'd like some time alone with her."

"No."

"No?"

Rather than give me an explanation, he lowers his eyes once more to stare at his daughter.

Sighing, I move to the other side of the incubator. I don't miss the way Duck tracks my movements without lifting his head or the way his shoulders seem to relax when he realizes I'm not leaving him alone.

"Have the doctors talked to you about her condition?" I ask, needing to fill the silence.

Duck shakes his head.

"Well, as you know, she's a preemie." I lift up the chart attached to the end of the incubator to read some of the information for him. "At birth, she weighed 1 pound 8 ounces and was just shy of 9 inches long. Her lungs are still developing, which is why she needs help breathing. She's—"

"Is she gonna die?"

"Excuse me?"

"Is my daughter going to die?" he asks.

"I, um..." I want to tell him no, to reassure him that she

will in fact live and be strong and healthy. But that would be a lie. "Honestly, I don't know."

"What do you mean you don't know? Isn't it your job to know?"

"If I could save lives simply by wishing it so, there would be no death in this hospital. But that's not how it works." I take a deep breath and blow it out slowly before continuing. "At twenty-five weeks, your daughter is what we call a micro-preemie. The odds of survival are around sixty to seventy percent. What that means is, there's a better chance of her making it than not."

"Yeah, no shit," he snaps. "I may look big and stupid, but I understand the odds."

Ignoring his words, I put the chart back where it belongs. "If you'd like to touch her, I can help get you gowned up and you can put your hands through these armholes." I point to the openings on either side of the incubator.

Duck stares at me for a minute before thumping the top of the plastic dome. "I'm good. I'm gonna head back downstairs."

He turns and strides toward the door, his spine stiff and his shoulders back. I rush to catch up with him, not sure what set him off, but when I grab his arm to stop him, he shakes me off.

"Don't ever touch me again," he snarls.

"I'm... Sorry."

I shove my hands in the pockets of my scrubs. I follow him down the hallway to the elevators and then silently ride with him back to the fifth floor. When we reach room five sixteen, he freezes.

"What are they doing?" he asks as he nods to the two men inside the room.

"It looks like they're cleaning up."

Duck whistles. "Look at you, queen of the fucking obvious."

My hackles rise. I'm tired of taking this man's shit. I know he's hurting, but that doesn't mean he has to bring everyone else down.

"I gotta go," he says flatly before turning and practically running to the elevator we stepped off of minutes ago.

He stabs his finger into the button with the down arrow and then crosses his arms over his chest. I try to ignore the way his muscles bulge under his shirt, but it's impossible. The man is equal parts infuriating and tempting, neither of which I have the time to indulge in.

Just as the doors slide open, I race to the elevator and get on... again.

"Why are you following me?"

"I'm not following you," I insist, although I very much am.

"Right."

"Does your daughter have a name?" I blurt. Duck's face loses color and simultaneously reddens. Huh... didn't realize that was possible. "The hospital needs to fill out a birth certificate, and they need her name to be able to do that."

"That's why you're following me?"

"I'm not following..." I shake my head. "Ya know what, it doesn't matter. Your daughter needs a name. We can't keep calling her Baby Smith."

Duck's body goes rigid. "Her last name is Howard, not Smith."

"And her first name?"

"I don't... we didn't..." Duck sighs. "I don't know."

"Well, did you have several names in mind?" I prod,

trying to help him figure this out. The man is feeling hope-less, or at least that's what I imagine he's feeling, and not being able to come up with a name for your child doesn't help.

"Daisy was the last one Heath... her mother and I agreed on." He lifts his gaze to meet mine. "What would you name her?"

"I... she's... um..."

"Never mind. She's not your daughter. Forget I asked."

"You're right, she's not." I stand there, awkwardly for a moment before spitting out, "I've always liked the name Lynn."

Duck nods. "Sounds good. Daisy Lynn Howard it is then."

"Right, well, good. I'll have them get that entered into the system and make sure her charts reflect her name."

"Thanks, um..." Duck chuckles ruefully. "I never did get your name."

"Grace. My name is Grace."

He looks like he wants to say something else, but the elevator doors slide open, and he takes off without a back-ward glance. I don't follow him this time. Instead, I lean back against the rail of the elevator and mentally berate myself for the last two minutes.

What the fuck was I thinking? I could have given him any name, so why is it I gave him the one name I hold sacred? The one name that rarely leaves my lips because it pains me to say it?

Why, oh why, did I give Duck my dead daughter's name and then feel a shiver down my spine at the way it sounded on his tongue?

CHAPTER 6
DUCK
TWO WEEKS LATER...

"You've reached—"

I disconnect the call and launch my phone at the wall. Heather has yet to answer any of my calls or texts. Although that shouldn't surprise me. She did tell me not to look for her. Then there's the fact that her apartment is empty and the hospital's security feed show's her leaving with an unknown man.

"Who pissed in your orange juice this morning?"

I whip my head up and see Grace striding through the door, hands on her hips and censure in her eyes.

"Why are you here?" I retort.

Grace drops her arms and sighs. "Same reason I'm here every morning. To make sure Daisy is okay while she's in here with you and not in the NICU."

Satan's Legacy pulled some strings—i.e. greased numerous palms, paid people off, bribed several hospital bigwigs—to make sure I was able to stay at the hospital with Daisy. I've been living in a patient room on the NICU floor for two weeks, despite not being able to bring myself to see Daisy every day.

"If that's why you're here, where is she?"

"Another nurse will be bringing her in soon."

I don't know why I'm goading her. She's been nothing but nice to me and supportive with Daisy. Maybe that's the problem. She's too fucking nice. I'm not in the right headspace for nice.

"You don't have to be here every time I'm with Daisy."

"And you're forgetting that your club ensured that I do," she snaps.

We've had this argument on a few different occasions. I don't want her here and she doesn't want to be here. But my brothers made sure neither of us had a choice in the matter.

Grace busies herself with picking up the pieces of my now broken phone. I should tell her to stop, that I'll do it, but I can't. Because as infuriating as she is and as much as I want nothing to do with her, I'm equally captivated by the way her scrubs hug her ass when she squats down, the curve of her hips, and the nape of her neck that's bare because she swept her hair up into a messy bun.

It's impossible to ignore her natural beauty. Trust me, I've tried. But the more time she spends in such close proximity, the harder it becomes. Despite my heart begging me to.

"Take a picture. It lasts longer."

I shake my head to scramble the path my thoughts were traveling, but before I can come up with a response, another nurse walks in the room pushing Daisy in her incubator. My eyes are immediately drawn to my daughter, but I'm ridiculously aware of how Grace and this nurse interact.

"You okay chicky?" he asks her.

She stands up with pieces of my phone in her hands and faces him. "Fine, why?"

He darts his gaze from her to me and back again. "You're not a maid, Grace. You don't have to clean up his messes."

Grace walks to the trash can and tosses my cell. Then she strides back to the man and wraps her arms around his neck.

"I'm good." She smacks a kiss on his cheek. "Promise."

He swats her ass and takes a step back before resting his hands on her shoulders and bending to be at eye level with her.

"It sucks dick not having you down in the pit."

Grace laughs, and the sound goes straight to my balls. The rest of me, however, is a jumbled mess of jealousy and disgust. How can I have this reaction to a woman who I don't even like, especially after what Heather did?

Because you're hurt and pissed, not dead.

"I'll be back before you know it," Grace assures him.

"Don't stay away on my account," I snap. "Wouldn't want to interfere with a workplace hookup."

Grace's eyes darken and she juts her chin. But it's her fuckboy who speaks.

"I know you think you can come in here and do whatever you want because your club has money, but you can't. Grace has given up a lot so she can be here for you, despite how you treat her."

I arch a brow in an effort to intimidate him. The little shit doesn't even seem fazed, which fuels the fire in my gut.

"Don't you need to get back to wherever the hell you crawled out of?"

"Duck," Grace admonishes. Her tone is a mixture of anger and horror. "Stop being an asshole."

"I'll stop being an asshole when he leaves. I don't

appreciate him coming into my space and getting all handsy with you."

"He wasn't getting handsy," she argues before turning to her friend. "Vince, just go."

"I don't think so, chicky."

"Please?" she pleads. "I'll make sure to get outta here at a decent time tonight and we can go out for drinks. How's that sound?"

Vince seems to think about it before he nods. "Fine, but only if you promise to go home first and shower. You haven't been home in two weeks and it's starting to show."

A red flush creeps up Grace's neck. "I've showered every single day."

"Showering at the hospital isn't the same thing."

Grace huffs out a breath. "Fine, I will. Now go."

Vince kisses her on the cheek and then disappears into the hallway, closing the door behind him. As soon as it clicks shut, Grace is rounding on me and jabs a finger into my chest.

"What the hell was that?!"

"What?"

Grace puffs out her chest and squares her shoulders. "Me big strong Tarzan, you no touch little Jane." She keeps her voice low, mocking. It's fucking adorable.

I don't bother to hide my grin. Hell, it would be impossible to. "I don't know what you're talking about."

And therein lies the problem, because I know exactly what she's talking about. That thought has me sobering real quick and focusing all my attention on Daisy.

"What's the report this morning?" I ask her, needing to change the subject.

Grace throws her hands up in the air and shakes her head. "You're impossible."

"So I've been told."

"Maybe you should do something about it then," she mumbles.

"Yeah, not gonna happen today so let's move on. Report?"

Grace rubs her temples as if I'm giving her a headache. Aw, poor thing. At least she can rub that. I've got an ache somewhere else that I can't do a damn thing about.

"Daisy is progressing as she should be. Other than that..." She shrugs. "The doctor said he'd be in to talk to you at some point today."

I gently roll the incubator toward the extremely uncomfortable chair in the room so I can sit and watch my little girl.

"You wanna touch her?" Grace asks.

She asks me this every day and every day I give her the same answer.

"No."

"Why?"

That's new.

I shrug, not having a ready answer.

"Bullshit," she snaps as she walks over to stand on the opposite side of Daisy. "I watch the way you look at her, the way your eyes plead with the universe to make her better. Why are you denying yourself, and her, of the comfort touching her can provide?"

I stiffen at her words, hating that she reads me so well. I know some may think I'm a bad father and a shitty human being. And they'd be right. I love my daughter more than anything. I feel a protectiveness toward her that is unlike anything I've ever felt. But that's exactly why I don't touch Daisy. I have the power to break her even when I don't want to.

"Duck, talk to me."

I lift my head so I can look Grace in the eye. "I don't want to hurt her."

Grace's face falls, a look of pity flashes over her features, making me wince. "You won't hurt her, I promise."

"That's not a promise you can make."

"Take off your shirt," she demands.

"Excuse me?"

"Oh stop it," she quips. "You heard me."

Interested in seeing where she's going with this, I do as she says, but I put my cut back on, feeling too exposed without it.

Grace fiddles with the incubator until it opens, and she reaches inside to lift Daisy into her arms. My heart bleeds at the sight of my baby girl in the arms of a woman who isn't her mother. Or at least that's the reason I tell myself because admitting that the bleed is from my heart cracking open is a harder pill to swallow.

When Grace turns to me, she rolls her eyes. "Would you relax? Sit back in the chair and breathe."

Only when she points it out do I realize I'm coiled tighter than a boa constrictor surrounding its prey. I force myself to take several deep breaths to calm my racing heart.

Completely oblivious to my discomfort, at least I think she is, Grace settles Daisy against my chest. I flinch at the contact, but my arms immediately cradle her. Somehow, my body instinctively knows what to do.

I gaze down into Daisy's perfect blue eyes, and the hatred and rage I've been carrying starts to melt. Don't get me wrong, I'm terrified I'll hurt her somehow, but I'm equally sure that I'll do anything I can to not let that happen.

When I look up at Grace, she's holding her phone out in front of her and tears are gathering in her eyes.

"What's wrong?"

She shakes her head vigorously before wiping away the evidence that there is indeed something wrong.

"Nothing. I, uh, was just taking a few pictures." Grace swallows. "I figured you might want them and since you broke your phone..." She shrugs.

She's lying, but I don't call her on it. Not because I don't want to drag the truth behind the tears out of her, but because my gut tells me that whatever it is is huge and knowing it will make me feel like protecting her.

"Oh, thanks."

Grace shoves her phone back into the pocket in her scrubs shirt and nods toward Daisy. "Skin-to-skin contact is good for her. Good for you too. Sometimes just being this close soothes the soul and allows the body to focus on healing."

"Makes sense."

"And whaddya know, you're not hurting her at all."

I know she's trying to make a joke, but it falls flat.

"Not all pain is physical."

She averts her gaze and starts to fidget with her hands. "No, it's not."

Again, the feeling that she's hiding something takes a hold of me.

No, stop caring. That's what got you to single father status.

I glance at the clock on the wall and grimace when I see that it's almost eleven o'clock. My brothers will be here any minute.

"I think it's time to take Daisy back to the NICU," I tell her.

"Are you sure? She can be here a little longer."

"Yeah, my club will be here soon, and I need to give them my full attention."

"If you say so."

Grace lifts Daisy out of my arms and places her back in the incubator. Daisy cries for a few seconds but when Grace begins to hum, she settles down. Fuck, I settle down.

Needing to put some emotional distance between me and the two females in the room, I focus on putting my shirt back on and the upcoming meeting. This hospital room isn't the best place for church, but with me not willing to leave, Snow caved and agreed to it for me.

"I'll bring her back this afternoon," Grace says as she's wheeling my daughter away.

"I'll be here."

"I know."

I don't even have time to process the last half hour or so because a minute later, Snow walks into the room. The others trail behind him, each of them wearing an expression that I've missed. It's the one that says we're about to fuck some shit up.

Good. I could use a little violence in my life right about now. A grin spreads on my face, but I can feel the evilness behind it. This day just keeps getting better and better.

"Hey, bros," I say. "Looks like I'm gonna be taking a little road trip."

CHAPTER 7

GRACE

I stare at my reflection, hardly recognizing the woman in the mirror. If you would've asked me two weeks ago who I was, I'd have proudly, and readily, answered that I'm a nurse who loves her job, a friend who is loyal, and a woman who knows what she does and doesn't want. Ask me the same thing today, and I don't have a clue how I'd answer.

Two weeks. That's all it took for Duck to get under my skin and securely insert himself into every fiber of my being. And it pisses me off to no end.

I walk to my dresser and pick up the note I'd found on the table in his room earlier this afternoon when I brought Daisy to see him. Rereading the words, heat curls around me, and not the good kind.

I had club business to handle. I'll see Daisy tomorrow.

Ten words is all Duck had written, but in those ten words, he made it very clear what his priorities are. I thought he'd made progress this morning when he engaged in skin-to-skin contact with Daisy, but I guess I was wrong.

I set the note back on my dresser and go about getting dressed. I'm meeting Vince and Lucy at our usual spot, but for reasons I don't want to analyze, I dress in clothes I wouldn't normally wear. The dark wash of my jeans pairs nicely with the emerald green halter top, and I finish it off with a fitting black leather jacket. My knee-high black boots with the three-inch heels make me feel sexy.

I grab the note again to fold it up and put it in my pocket. I'm staying at the hospital tonight, and I plan on confronting Duck with it.

Making my way through my apartment toward the door, I flip off lights and then snag my keys and purse off the table in the entryway. I lock up and head for my car.

The drive to the bar goes by in a blur because my mind races with thoughts of Duck. How is it possible for a man to infuriate me and turn me on at the same time? Because he does. There are times when he's so dismissive of me, so annoyingly gruff, that all I want to do is kiss him to shut him the hell up.

Fuck Duck. Don't let him ruin your night.

I step inside the bar and am charged by Vince and Lucy almost immediately.

"I thought for sure you'd back out," Lucy says, loud enough to be heard over the music. "You've been spending all your free time with Mr. Howard, it's almost as if you've forgotten us."

My hackles rise at that statement, already on edge when it comes to anything Duck related. "In case you've forgotten, I haven't had a choice in how much time I spend with him. His club threw a lot of money at the hospital to ensure that was the case. Until his daughter is discharged, I'm assigned to them and only them."

Lucy's eyes flash hurt, but she quickly masks it. "I was just giving you a hard time."

"Lucy, trust me, that man does that enough," Vince chimes in, censure in his tone. "Grace doesn't need us to do it too."

I bump my shoulder into Vince, silently thanking him for sticking up for me. He winks back.

"Well, are we gonna stand here all night or drink?" I ask.

"Drink," Lucy says and practically drags me to the bar, leaving Vince to trail behind.

"How many shots are we doing tonight?"

I haven't been in the ER, so I'm totally out of the loop. I miss the ER, sure, but it's been kinda nice not to face death every single day. But I've traded one monster for another.

"I had five ODs," Lucy says.

"I had four deaths, two of which were ODs."

I whistle. "Damn. Is it that red pill with the bat bullshit, or something else?"

"Red pills all around."

"How does this keep happening?" I grumble. "Surely the police can track the supplier down and stop it."

"Yeah, well, if they can, they aren't," Vince snaps.

"What can I get ya?" a bartender I don't recognize asks once we belly up to the bar.

"We're gonna need twenty-seven shots of..." I glance at Lucy and Vince to see what they want, but they both shrug. "Twenty-seven shots of Jack Daniels and a pitcher of whatever ya got on tap."

The bartender arches a brow. "Twenty-seven shots?"

Vince pushes up next to me and smiles at the bartender.

"Yeah, sugar, twenty-seven. Think you can handle that, or do you need me to come back there and assist you?"

"If I weren't on the clock, I might just take you up on that, but as it stands, I'm working," the bartender dead-pans. "And I don't think the question is whether or not *I* can handle that many shots. The more appropriate question is, can *you*?"

"Just pour and sit back and watch," Vince counters.

There's so much sexual tension in their extremely short exchange that I feel like a voyeur at a porn flick taping.

"I think I will," the bartender says. "Why don't you all go find a table and I'll have a waitress bring you everything?"

"Thanks."

I turn and lead my friends to a small table in the corner of the bar. It's not lost on me that Vince takes the seat that gives him the best view of the bartender. No doubt they'll be eye fucking all night long.

An image of Duck pops in my head, and it remains there until a waitress brings our alcohol and I'm able to down two shots in quick succession.

"Damn, chicky, slow down," Vince teases. "You'll be passed the fuck out before we even get started."

I ignore him and down my third shot for good measure. After that and half a glass of beer, I'm feeling pretty damn good, in an on-my-way-to-drunktown sorta way.

Two hours and a lot of dancing later, Lucy calls it a night. Vince walks her out so she doesn't have to wait for her Uber alone, and when he returns, he practically flops into his chair.

"Ah, that bitch is exhausting," he mutters, lifting his last shot and downing it.

"But we love her."

"I'd love her more if she'd stop giving you such a hard time about shit," he counters. "I'm starting to feel like my friendship with her is more about keeping my friends close but my enemies closer than any real affection."

"I can handle everything she throws at me, Vince. I'm a big girl."

"Didn't look like you were handling her whole 'find a man to suck and fuck and you'll feel better' routine." Vince leans forward to rest his chin in his palm. "In fact, it looked like you wanted to strangle her."

I flap my hand to dismiss his claim and ignore the image of me kneeling in front of Duck that flashes in my mind, same way I did when Lucy said it.

"I didn't want to strangle her," I say. "Ugh, is it hot in here or is it just me?" I fan my face, hoping like hell he can't see the flush I can feel.

Unfortunately, Vince sees all, and sits up a little straighter. "Oh my God."

"What?"

He points at my face. "Your eyes."

"What about my eyes?"

"They're a little brighter, just like they were every single time Duck was mentioned tonight." Vince grins. "You actually like the asshole."

"Of course, I don't like him. He's infuriating."

"That might be true, but it doesn't change the facts. You like him. And more than that, you wanna bang him into next year."

I wince at that. Giving myself time to come up with a retort, I polish off my last two shots.

"See." Vince claps like he's figured out the secret to living forever. "You can't even come up with an argument. You might not want to like him, but you do."

I stand, pushing my chair back as I do, and wobble. Gripping the edge of the table, I take a moment to steady myself. Once I feel like I can walk without toppling over, I start toward the door. Vince is beside me in a flash.

"You're mad."

"No, I'm not," I assure him.

We walk in silence until we're outside and I've called for an Uber.

"You know I just want you to be happy, right?"

I turn to Vince and smile. Or at least I think I smile. It's hard to tell from within the vat of liquor that seems to have replaced every drop of blood in my body.

"I know."

"Do you? Because it feels a little like you're punishing yourself for what happened five years ago."

Tears gather in my eyes at that. "For argument's sake, let's say I agree that I deserve to be happy. The last person I would open myself up to is that... that..." I stomp my foot like a teenager. "That self-centered, arrogant, broody... insanely hot man."

"Or maybe that's exactly who you should open yourself up to." He holds up a hand when I open my mouth to protest. "Look, all I'm saying is we can't control who we like. Sometimes it just happens when we least expect it. Sure, maybe you'd get hurt or heartbroken or whatever, but isn't it worth a shot? Because maybe, just maybe, you wouldn't get hurt. Maybe you'd get healed."

"Stuff it, oh wise one," I snark.

"Fine, stuffing it."

My Uber pulls up and as I'm sliding very ungracefully into the back seat, Vince calls out. "I'll check on you in the morning. Try to get some sleep."

I'm not able to respond because I shut my door and the

driver takes off toward the hospital. It's only a few blocks away, and when we arrive, I get out of the car and stumble along through the ER entrance. I don't make eye contact with anyone because I'm not in the mood for their judgment or questions.

Yes, I'm three sheets to the wind. Yes, I'm technically at work. But no, I don't give a rat's ass.

When I reach the NICU floor, I bypass checking on Daisy, as it wouldn't do a bit of good in my current state. Instead, I march past it and toward the room that Duck's been living in. By the time I reach the door, I've worked up quite the temper and am prepared to throw it at him full force.

But then I open the door and freeze. The room is empty. The man still isn't back from his 'club business', whatever the hell that means. I pull Duck's earlier note out of my pocket and stare at it as if it will tell me what I want to know, as if it somehow holds the answer to where he's at and what the hell he's up to.

Spoiler alert, it doesn't.

Rather than try to make it to the room the hospital is letting me stay in, I shuffle to the bed and fall face first into the mattress, the note still clenched in my hand. I may not be able to yell at him or ask my questions right now, but mark my words, the second he walks in the room, it's on.

CHAPTER 8
DUCK

Leaving the hospital was much harder than I thought it would be. I'd stupidly believed that I'd be able to walk out the doors and enter the world I'm used to, the one where I'm the VP of a one percenter motorcycle club, and it would feel normal, natural. But I hadn't counted on a piece of my heart staying behind with Daisy.

Which is why the punk hanging from the ceiling of our torture shed is bloodier than he should be at this point. I need to get this done so I can get back to my baby.

I lift my leg and kick him in the balls before landing an uppercut to his jaw. Blood spurts from his mouth and his head lolls to the side.

"Motherfucker," I seethe, wrapping a hand around his throat. "You're gonna tell us what we want to know. One way or another, I'll break you for the information."

Bubba—which is a ridiculous name for the scrawny fuck—smiles, revealing blood coated rotting teeth. He may have been driving the truck that caused Heather's accident, but someone paid him to do it.

Our resident tech guy was able to hack into all the traffic cameras and find an image that he could run through facial recognition software. More than that, he cross-referenced Bubba's bank accounts and found a deposit of ten grand, but he was unable to trace the source.

"Who paid you?" I ask Bubba for what feels like the millionth time.

He says nothing.

Magic, our Enforcer, steps up beside me. He and I are the only brothers in the shed, as the rest went home hours ago knowing we'd finish the job. Answers or death are the only ways this ends, preferably both.

Magic lifts the sledgehammer in his hand and matches Bubba's wicked grin. "You better start talking."

Bubba remains silent. The cracking of bone fills the space as Magic delivers blows to both the idiot's kneecaps.

"Who. Paid. You?" Magic sneers.

"It doesn't matter!" Bubba shouts, crimson droplets shooting from his lips.

I plunge my knife into his thigh, and he screams in agony. "It matters." I yank the blade free and wipe it clean on my jeans.

Bubba begins to babble, his words and sentences incoherent behind the pain and fear in his voice.

"I can't understand you," Magic singsongs as he lifts the sledgehammer.

"It d-doesn't matter b-because he's a g-ghost."

"What's that supposed to mean?"

"It m-means, you'll n-never find him. I d-don't have a name and n-never saw him in p-person."

I look to Magic. "You believe him?"

Magic darts his eyes to Bubba and then back to me. "Unfortunately, yes."

"Me too."

Bubba swings his legs a little. "So, y-you're gonna let m-me go?"

Magic tsks Bubba and focuses on me. "It's your call, VP."

I pretend to give it a lot of thought, enjoying the way it makes Bubba squirm and mindlessly plead for his life. He really is an idiot if he thinks he's walking out of here.

"Ya know what?" I smile at both of them. "I think good ol' Bubba here deserves to be rewarded for his cooperation."

"Any ideas of what type of reward he should get?" Magic asks.

I glance at Bubba and revel in the hope flashing in his eyes. He genuinely believes he's being rewarded. I'd almost feel bad for the guy if... yeah, there's nothing that would make me feel bad for him. Fucker decided to play with the big dogs but failed to remember he's only a weak little puppy.

Without hesitation, I plunge my knife into the bastard's gut and yank it upward, focusing on the way the hope, and the life, drains from his eyes. Once his body is limp, I pull the knife out and again, wipe it clean on my jeans.

"Great reward," Magic huffs out with a laugh.

I shrug. "I thought so." I slide my knife back into my boot before taking in the scene. "This place is a mess. I'd love to help clean up but—

"You've got a daughter to get back to," he finishes for me and claps me on the back. "You off your game a bit, bro. You seem to be forgetting that this place is self-cleaning."

Fuck, I did forget... but only for the space of time it took for my mind to go from vicious thoughts of revenge to my baby girl.

"Bite me," I snap.

"Eh, I'd rather go home and bite my wife, then spend the rest of the pre-dawn hours sucking and licking until she's begging for more."

"Don't let Snow here you talk about his little sister like that."

"Bro, he's got no room to talk. He and Sami go at it like rabbits."

"Fine, don't listen. It's your dick on the line."

Magic rolls his eyes at me and chuckles, but there's a nervous quality to it because he knows I'm right. Snow may be on board with Magic and Laney's marriage now, but there was a time he wasn't so thrilled.

Once outside the shed, I barricade the dead man inside with the wooden latch and then nod to Magic. He pulls on the single piece of wood that sets everything on the inside of the steel vault beneath the ramshackle shed ablaze. We take turns watching through the knot hole, ensuring that Bubba burns.

Once he's as ashy as he's going to get and the flames die down, the floor opens up to swallow every shred of evidence into the pit below. Satisfied that we're done here, we both grab our cuts from the tree branch and slide them on before making our way back toward the compound.

"We really didn't get much out of him," Magic comments.

"He didn't have anything useful to give us. I meant it when I said I believe he never got a name or saw a face."

"I did too."

"I need to head back to the hospital, but I've got my laptop there, so I'll keep digging. I'll also let Snow know to have our tech guy do the same. Between text messages and that money trail, something's bound to reveal whoever the fuck is behind this."

"Agreed." Magic slaps me on the back. "You do know though, that finding this guy isn't gonna change things with Heather, right? Because that footage of her leaving the hospital with another man is telling."

I snort. "No shit. I don't want the bitch back." I shove a hand through my hair. "I'll admit that at first, I would've given anything to have her walk through the door, but now, having seen that hospital security footage, and her consistently ignoring my calls... I want answers, but I sure as shit don't want her."

"What about Daisy?"

"What about her?"

"If Heather shows her face again, would you let her see Daisy?"

That's a damn good question. One I hadn't really thought about until now. I certainly don't want to hurt Daisy by keeping her mother from her, but I also don't want her to experience the pain that comes from having a mother who doesn't want her.

"I don't know," I finally answer honestly.

"Maybe you should ask that sexy nurse Snow managed to get assigned to Daisy's medical team, get her opinion." Magic bumps his shoulder into mine, chuckling as he does.

At the mention of Grace, my cock reacts immediately, pressing against my zipper almost to the point of pain.

"Why the fuck would I do that?" I ask.

Magic points to my crotch. "Because just having her mentioned does that shit to you."

I shove Magic forward when we reach the back of the house he shares with Laney and the kids.

"You're a dumbass, bro," I accuse. "The last thing I need

right now is a woman in my life to fuck shit up." I shake my head. "Nah, not after Heather."

"Your call, D. But for the record, you're allowed to move on."

After only two weeks?

"I'm good."

"Maybe, but cold showers only get ya so far."

"Jesus, let it go," I snap, annoyed with his pushing.

Magic raises his hands in front of him and starts to walk backward toward his back door. "I'll let it go for now."

"Thanks." Sarcasm drips from my tone, but Magic doesn't comment on it.

"Give that baby a hug from her Uncle Magic when you see her in the morning."

I chuckle at that because all of my brothers have deemed themselves Daisy's uncles. Not that I'm complaining. They're family and she will always have them around to love and protect her. And likely spoil her rotten.

"Go fuck your wife, Magic," I call out to him after he opens the door.

"Oh, I plan on it."

Shaking my head, I stroll toward the clubhouse at the front of the compound. I left my Harley there so we could take the van to pick up Bubba. I straddle the seat and fire her up, letting the vibrations rattle through me.

The ride to the hospital goes by too fast. One minute, I'm leaving Satan's Legacy property and the next, I'm in the hospital parking lot searching for Grace's car. When I don't spot it, anger flares. She's supposed to be here, watching over Daisy.

She can't work twenty-four-seven.

And even though I know this, I can't stop my frustration from bubbling up. I stride toward the entrance and quickly make my way up to my room. The entire time I'm thinking of all the things I want to say to Grace, ways to convey my building fury at her complete disregard for her duties.

I pass Grace's room first and see that it's empty. Glancing at my phone, I see it's four in the morning.

Where the fuck is she?

I force myself to breathe, in and out, in and out. My tirade will have to wait until later since she can't even be bothered to be here. When I reach my room, the door is shut, so I push it open and freeze.

Because curled up in a fetal position on my bed is Grace. I quietly walk to the bed and stare down at her, all of my anger fading into the background. Beneath her closed eyelids, her eyes are frantically darting back and forth, indicative of a nightmare in progress.

I don't know what comes over me, but I reach down and push a strand of hair off her forehead. She whimpers in her sleep, and just like that, all the reasons I had for wanting nothing to do with her dissipate under an intense need to protect her, to take away whatever pain caused her current situation.

Son of a bitch.

CHAPTER 9
GRACE

"Get out."

I stare out the passenger window at the rundown apartment building Carter parked in front of. This isn't home and after everything that's happened in the last forty-eight hours, I just want to go home.

"Take me home," I say quietly, not bothering to look at my fiancé.

"This is home, Grace," he sneers. "Now get the fuck outta my car."

I shake my head, which dislodges the tears I've been fighting. I already lost my daughter, I refuse to lose my relationship and home too. Pain spreads across my face when Carter backhands me.

"I said get out!"

What is happening? Carter's never hurt me before, not physically anyway. He's perfected inflicting emotional pain in the last two days, but I've chalked it up to his anguish over losing Lynn. My brain knows that's not an excuse. But my heart? That's another matter. It's already broken, and I'll do anything to keep it from disintegrating further.

"Why are you doing this?"

"Seriously?" Carter chuckles, but it sounds more evil than funny. "Your body killed our kid." I wince at the reminder. "And you've been so deep in your head since you pushed her out you haven't even noticed that your ring is missing." I glance at my hands, shocked to see he's right. My engagement ring is gone. "Don't worry, I've got it. But mark my words, Grace, you will never wear it again. You and I are done."

A sob breaks free, and I cover my mouth to contain the sobs that threaten to follow. Apparently, Carter gets tired of waiting for me to do his bidding, because he gets out of the car, slamming the door behind him. He stalks around the hood and yanks open the passenger door.

"C'mon," he says as he grabs my arm and hauls me out of the vehicle.

I stumble, but he doesn't bother to steady me. He simply keeps dragging me toward the building entrance. When we step inside, I try to pull free of his painful grasp, but he holds me tight.

There doesn't appear to be an elevator and when Carter leads me up a stairwell, not giving a damn that I'm tripping over every other step just to keep up, my thought is confirmed. Four flights of stairs later, he shoves open a door and drags me down the dingy hallway, coming to a stop in front of a door that reads four-ten.

Carter pulls a key out of his pocket and shoves it in the lock. When it disengages, he opens the door and pushes me inside. If his behavior up until this point was shocking, it has nothing on the bewilderment I experience when I see boxes scattered throughout the living room.

"All your shit is here, so you have no reason to come back to the condo," he tells me, his tone void of any emotion. "I know I can't keep you from the memorial service for Lynn, but other *than that, I don't ever want to see your face again, Grace. Got it?"*

Numbly, I nod. Carter's hand slices across my cheek, which enhances the pain I already have from the first slap.

"You're not mute, Grace. Use your goddamn words."

"I... I g-got it," I sob.

"Good." Carter holds out the key he used to open the door and drops it on the floor in front of me. "There's your key."

Without another word, he walks out the door, slamming it behind him. Unable to hold myself upright any longer, I collapse to the floor and pull myself into a fetal position. Wracking sobs tear through my body as I recount every single moment from the time Carter took me to the hospital because I was in labor to him walking out the door a few minutes ago.

I don't know how long I lay there, but it feels like hours before the crying stops and I force myself to get up. I shuffle through the apartment until I find the bathroom. Flipping the light on, I wince at the brightness and then gasp when I see my reflection.

My cheeks are red from Carter's blows and my eyes are bloodshot and dull. I see no trace of the woman who was so happy a short time ago, who thought she had a wonderful life ahead of her. No, all I see is a broken shell of a human whose entire world crashed and burned, all because of something she couldn't control.

I haul my arm back and ram it into the glass, further shattering the woman staring back at me. Blood trickles down my hand, but I feel no pain, even though there are shards of glass sticking out of my knuckles.

Throwing my head back, I scream, the sound reverberating in the tiny room, threatening to swallow me up and spit me back out on the other side of reality, the other side where my daughter would be waiting for me.

I jackknife into a sitting position, wildly swinging my arms to break free from the hands trying to hold me still.

"Get off me," I cry out. "Just let me die."

"Grace," a voice snaps. I continue my struggle until I'm pulled tightly against a hard chest and strong arms wrap around me. "Grace, it's me. It's Duck."

Duck?

For some reason, this man's arms ground me back into reality, allowing me to give in to the utter despair my nightmares always cause. My body goes limp as sobs erupt from deep within.

"Shhh, it's okay," Duck croons. "You're safe."

I may not be in physical danger, but I'm far from safe.

After a while, my tears begin to slow, and I become totally aware of the heat surrounding me. I push back from Duck and swipe the wetness from my cheeks. Now that there's space between us, there's room for humiliation to sneak its way in.

Nausea swirls in my gut. I slap a hand over my mouth and race to the bathroom, slamming the door behind me. I manage to drop in front of the toilet just in time to empty my stomach. My head throbs and my throat burns by the time I've purged all the alcohol and embarrassment.

I slump back against the wall, drawing my knees up to my chest. There's a soft knock on the door, but I ignore it. I didn't lock the thing, so he could come in if he wanted to, but I'm hoping he doesn't.

"Grace, are you okay?" Duck calls through the door.

"Fine," I croak. "I'll be out in a minute."

He doesn't respond, but I hear his footsteps as he walks away from the bathroom.

Leaning my head back against the wall, I raise my eyes

toward the heavens and whisper, "I miss you, baby girl. Someday I'll be with you."

But not today.

I push myself to my feet and turn on the faucet. Splashing water on my face, I avoid my reflection. But when I grab Duck's tube of toothpaste and put a dab on my finger, it's impossible to ignore. My eyes remind me of that day, all those years ago, when I looked at my mirrored image. All the pain and rage from that time surges through me and before I know it, my hand is smashing into the glass.

Welcoming the pain my action brings, I let it feed the hollow places inside of me. All those places I thought I was doing a damn good job ignoring... until a man and his baby came along and forced those places into the light, reminding me of everything I lost.

I make quick work of scrubbing my teeth with the toothpaste before I focus on rinsing the blood from my other hand. There are several tiny pieces of glass embedded in my skin, so I gingerly pick those out, sucking air between my teeth at the sting. Once that's done, I grab several paper towels and wrap them around the wounds.

I fully expected Duck to storm into the bathroom when he heard glass breaking, so I'm surprised to see him sitting in the chair in the corner of the room when I open the door and step out.

His eyes travel from my face down to my wrapped hand, which is now sporting bloody paper towels. I take advantage of his perusal and do some looking of my own. Duck's shirt is covered in dried blood, and there are crimson splatters covering his face and arms. When he meets my gaze again, he cocks a brow.

"Feel better?"

Rather than answer his question, I counter it with one

of my own. "What happened to you? Where were you last night?"

"Excuse me?" he says, slowly rising from the chair and stalking toward me.

I square my shoulders. "You left yesterday rather than see Daisy, so I'm wondering... what was so damn important that it supersedes your daughter and causes that much filth?" I point at his dirty clothes.

He nods toward the crumpled piece of paper that's on the mattress, where I must have dropped it in my sleep. "Like the note said, club business."

"What does that even mean?"

"It means it's none of *your* fucking business." Duck steps closer, his stare hard and unforgiving. "What were you dreaming about?"

"None of *your* fucking business," I snap, throwing his words back at him.

"You made it my business when you passed out in my bed," he snarls and wraps his fingers around my throat. I should be scared, but I'm not because I instinctively know he won't hurt me. "You made it my business when you sobbed into my chest and let me hold you."

Duck's eyes are swirling pools of... well, I don't really know what. But it's different, darker, more lustful. His stare burrows into me, burning a path all the way to my pussy, which is clenching at the way he's touching me.

Don't cave, Grace. You're angry. Hold onto that.

"You have two seconds to take your hand off of me before I start screaming loud enough to raise the dead."

He hesitates for a second before lowering his arm. "Get out of my room," he commands.

"Or what?"

Duck's nostrils flare. "Or I'll be forced to show you exactly who you're dealing with."

My nipples harden at his threat. My head realizes that my body's reaction is ridiculous, but my body is ignoring the memo.

"You, *Mr. Howard*, are an asshole."

Without another word, I stomp out of the room and down the hall, seeking the safety of my own temporary space. I snag a few necessary items from the cart in the room before locking myself in the bathroom.

Cleaning my wounded hand again, I force thoughts of Duck out of my mind. The man is the epitome of arrogance. He's annoying, hurtful, dangerous, and so fucking broken in a way that makes me want to put him back together again.

CHAPTER 10

DUCK

How can the itty-bitty human in my arms fill my heart so full of love? Especially when my soul denies the idea of love like an addict denies having a problem. It makes no sense, but it's true.

Daisy's lungs have developed to the point where she can breathe on her own, but she's still too small to go home. So, other than the IV that's pumping her full of nutrients, she's the tiniest bundle of perfection I've ever seen.

Grace brought Daisy in about an hour ago, but she has yet to say anything more than 'take your shirt off'. For a split second, my cock started to harden at the thought of getting to feel her up close and personal, but then she lifted Daisy from the incubator and all sexual thoughts flew out the window. She placed my daughter on my chest for more skin-to-skin time and then moved to stand by the door where she's currently doing something on her phone.

An alarm beeps and Grace pushes away from the doorframe to cross the room to me. My arms tighten around

Daisy, knowing that she's about to be returned to the NICU. I don't want to let her go, but I know I have to.

"Time's up," Grace says as she lifts Daisy into her arms. "I'll bring her back this afternoon."

I stand to put my shirt back on as I watch Daisy be lowered into the incubator. As Grace wheels her out of the room, her pager goes off. She pauses to look at it.

"Shit."

"What?" I move to stand closer to her, but not too close.

"Nothing. I'm needed in the pit."

She leaves then, not giving me any more information. Not that I expected her to, not after our argument earlier.

Ten minutes later, Snow, Magic, Toga, and Dip stroll through the door, scowls on their faces.

"What's up?" I ask, suddenly on alert.

"You should see it downstairs, bro," Toga states. "Fucking zoo."

"It's an ER," I remind him. "It's bound to get crazy."

"Not like this," Snow snaps. "They're dealing with overdose after overdose. And I noticed several baggies of those fucking red pills at the nurse's station."

My mind flashes to Grace and the page she got. "Motherfucker."

"Exactly." Magic crosses his arms over his chest. "This Dracula prick doesn't seem to give a shit about the lives he's destroying. At least we make sure the product is clean before we distribute it. And we don't deal to kids or soccer moms. He doesn't seem to have the same conscience."

"Most dealers don't," Dip says. "But Dracula's different."

"How so?" Snow asks.

"I don't know," Dip admits as he scratches his head.

"This feels personal somehow. I mean, he's the first dealer we haven't been able to track down, the only one who seems to have gotten into the fabric of this city. And he's escalating."

"Is he escalating, or does he simply have more clients now, so the death toll is naturally rising?"

Snow shakes his head. "This is a clusterfuck, that's for sure. Whatever this guy's end game is, he's proven that he's not going anywhere and will do whatever he has to in order to achieve his goal."

"Yeah, but what he doesn't know is we'll do the same," Magic grates out. "We don't stop until he's found and eliminated."

"Of course we wo—"

"Hello, gentlemen."

We all turn toward the door to see the doctor standing there, a tablet in his hand.

"Hi, Doc." I move to shake his hand. "Is something wrong? Is Daisy okay?"

"Mr. Howard, Daisy is doing fine," he assures me. "Which is why I wanted to talk to you. I'd like to start formulating a discharge plan. She still has to gain a little weight, but once she reaches our goal, she'll be able to go home. We find that it's a much smoother transition if everything necessary for her to thrive at home is already in place."

Immediately, my gut clenches. I knew that Daisy would be going home at some point, but now that it's close, fear holds me in its grip. What if I can't do this? What if I can't give her what she needs?

It's easy to forget that there's much more to parenting than skin-to-skin contact when you're holed up in a hospital and surrounded by people who know what they're doing. It's another matter entirely to realize you're gonna have to do it all alone.

"That's great news," Snow says when I remain silent. "We'll make sure that Daisy has whatever she needs."

"I'm sure you will," Doc responds, but he's focused on me. "Mr. Howard, is everything okay?"

Without thought, I blurt, "No. I mean, yes." I take a deep breath and nod. "Yes, everything is fine."

The doctor's eyebrows shoot up. "Are you sure?"

Snow rests his arm across my shoulders. "He's just nervous, Doc. But what single father of an infant isn't?"

Doc chuckles. "I have yet to see one who doesn't freak out, at least a little bit."

"We appreciate the update on Daisy," Magic says. "If you can give us a list of stuff she'll need, aside from the normal diapers, formula, bottles, and such, that'd be great. We'll make sure to have it all in place for when she's discharged."

"Right, well..." The doctor clears his throat. "I'll have Nurse Grace bring it with her when she brings Daisy back this afternoon."

"Uh, thanks," I finally find the presence of mind to say. "Appreciate it."

"No problem."

After he leaves, Snow moves to stand in front of me, placing his hands on my shoulders. "Look at me, D."

I lift my eyes to his.

"We've got your back, yeah?" I nod. "Good. Now stop thinking you're in this alone. Daisy has an entire club ready to help take care of her. You are not alone. Never forget that."

I see Toga's face fall out of the corner of my eye and my heart breaks for the dude. He and Fallon wouldn't have been alone either. Hell, they *aren't* alone, but he still chooses to bear the weight of their loss by himself.

I vow to trust in my brothers, their ol' ladies, to ensure I don't fall flat on my face when it comes to raising my daughter. And I vow to do whatever it takes to make sure none of them ever feel alone.

"None of us are alone," I say. "We're family, and I've never been more grateful for that than I am now."

"Damn straight." Snow slaps my back. "Now, back to business. We're still working hard on figuring out who Dracula is. Pretty sure we're close to tracing the money trail from the pissant who hit Heather though, so that's good."

"Speaking of the bitch," I say. "I've done some more digging. She's deleted all social media accounts, closed all of her bank accounts, and I can't find any utility bills associated with her name. It's like she never even existed."

"She can hide all she wants," Toga snaps. "We know she exists and will track her down eventually."

"He's right, we will. But in the meantime, we stay vigilant and be prepared for anything. Between the drugs, the bitch, and whoever paid Bubba to cause that crash, we can't afford to be anything less than one hundred percent on our game."

"Agreed."

"Okay, we're gonna head back to the compound. I'll call and check in later," Snow says as he makes his way to the door. "Maybe one of these days we'll get here in time to see your little munchkin. Until then, keep me posted on the list from the doctor and we'll take care of everything so you don't have to worry about it."

"I appreciate that, man."

"I know."

After our goodbyes, I flop onto the bed, wishing like hell it was my king-size mattress back home. As scared as I am to take Daisy home, I can't wait to get the fuck outta here.

CHAPTER 11
GRACE

As much as I love working in the ER, I don't miss days like this, days filled with death. I toss my gloves into the trash as I leave the bay that's now a temporary resting place for a deceased fourteen-year-old who took pills she had no business taking.

"Hey, girl."

I lift my head and see Lucy striding toward me. "Hey."

"I take it daddy and daughter went home."

"No, they're still here. I was paged to help with the overflow. But now that we're caught up, I'm heading back up to the NICU."

"You don't sound happy about that."

"It's not that, it's just..."

"Just what?" Lucy prods.

"She likes him," Vince says as he joins us.

Lucy's face lights up. "Oooh, are you gonna fuck him?"

I wince and her face falls as her eyes focus on something behind me.

"Don't let me stop you from answering."

76

I whip around and have to tip my head back to see Snow's eyes twinkling.

"I, um, I don't..." I heave a sigh. "This is... shit."

Snow chuckles before leveling his gaze on Lucy and Vince. "If you two don't mind, I need to speak with Grace." When they don't move, he tacks on, "Alone."

"Right. We'll talk to you later, chicky," Vince says, and he has to practically drag Lucy away because she's too nosy for her own good.

I rock back on my heels, suddenly feeling very claustrophobic around this giant of a man. It's weird, because I don't feel that way around Duck, who's equally big, but something about Snow commands attention and respect, not pussy clenching and attitude.

"Relax, Grace. I don't bite." He grins. "But Duck does, given the right circumstances."

Heat licks across my cheeks, and Snow's grin turns to a knowing smirk.

"I'm gonna take that reaction as a yes, you'd fuck my brother."

"Brother?" I squeak.

"Not by blood, of course. But yeah, he's my brother in every way that matters."

"Okay."

"Anyway, is there somewhere we can talk privately?"

I glance around me as if I'll find a space in the ER, but I know that's impossible. I decide to take him up to one of the surgical floors where there are small offices for the doctors to provide updates to family members.

Once we're both inside the small space, I clasp my hands in front of me. I don't bother sitting because I'm hoping we won't be in here that long.

"What's up?" I ask when he doesn't say anything.

"I have a proposition for you," he begins. "And before you say no, I need you to hear me out completely and keep an open mind."

"That sounds ominous."

Snow pinches the bridge of his nose. "Sorry. Unless I'm talking to Sami, I tend to not be all that great at conversation."

"Sami?"

"My wife."

"Ahh, okay." I shrug. "Listen, just spit out whatever it is you have to say, and I promise I'll keep an open mind. How's that sound?"

"Good."

"Okay, so..."

"I want you to move in with Duck and Daisy once Daisy's discharged."

I plop down into the chair with a thud, my legs unable to hold my weight a second longer. "You wh-what?"

"Shit, that was too blunt, wasn't it?"

"It was... well, I don't know what it was." I shake my head. "Not at all what I was expecting, I guess."

"Judging by how fast the color drained from your face, I don't doubt it."

I tilt my head and give him a 'ya think' look. And then I do the exact opposite of what I promised.

"No."

"You said you'd keep an open mind."

"Did you even talk to Duck about this?"

"No."

I huff out a breath. "Figures. Look, even if I agreed, Duck most certainly wouldn't. He hates me."

"Do you hate him?"

"Yes," I blurt, knowing it's a lie. I'm mad at the man, I don't hate him.

"Liar," Snow accuses. "You don't hate him any more than he hates you. And by that I mean there's something burning between the two of you but you're both too chicken shit to do anything about it. I've seen the way you look at each other during my visits, so don't try to deny it."

His words hit a little too close to home and my anger flares. And I refuse to feed into his theory.

"I can't move in with them."

"Why?"

That's the million-dollar question, isn't it? Technically, I could, but at what cost to myself? I can't imagine giving over the part of me that is hanging on to my own little girl or the even bigger part of me that's battered and damaged beyond repair.

"If it's a money thing, I'm prepared to pay you double what you make here."

My eyes bug at that. "Double? For what? To sleep there?"

"No, to live there. To leave your job and help Duck and Daisy full-time."

"Oh, hell no." I shoot up from my chair. "It's not gonna happen."

"Again, why?"

"I can tell you're not a man used to the word 'no', so allow me to dumb it down for you. N. O. No. Not happening. Will never happen." I enunciate the word again for good measure. "No."

"Why?"

"Jesus, you don't quit, do you?"

"Not in my DNA to quit." He smiles. "So, Grace... why?"

"Because it'll hurt too fucking much to say goodbye to another daughter!" I yell, tears springing to my eyes.

Shock settles into his expression. "You have a daughter?"

"Yes. No." I take a steadying breath but give up the battle to control my tears. "I did. She, um..."

Snow lifts a hand. "You don't have to tell me."

"No, I do. You asked me to be open-minded and you deserve to know why I'm not. I delivered my stillborn daughter, Lynn, five years ago and my life went to shit afterward. Suffice it to say, I'm not over it, and spending any more time with Daisy is just too much." I sink back into the chair, drawing my knees up to my chest.

He kneels in front of me and rests his hands on either side of me. "Grace, I can't even begin to understand what that's like. But..."

"Why is there always a but?" I grumble.

"You said your daughter's name was Lynn, right?"

"Yeah, so?"

"Daisy's middle name is Lynn."

"I know. Duck asked me for a name and that's what I suggested."

"Don't you think you're way past guarding yourself against any pain being around Duck and Daisy might bring? I mean, you've already helped to name her, you've taken on the role of caretaker for them here at the hospital. They're a part of your life no matter how hard you refuse to believe it."

Dammit! Why does he have to have a point?

"The fact remains, if I move in with them, I'm taking on that mother role with Daisy. I'll be playing the part of housewife only to be cast aside down the road when I'm no longer needed. And then what? Daisy will have two mothers who've abandoned her. That's not fair to her."

"And what if you aren't cast aside? What if it turns into something permanent?"

I narrow my eyes at Snow. "Are you trying to make sure Daisy's taken care of, or are you playing matchmaker?"

"Does it matter?" he counters.

I think about that for a moment and realize that, no, it doesn't. Because as hard as it will be to walk away down the road, I selfishly want whatever time I can have to live a normal life, like the one I was supposed to have.

"I have conditions," I say grudgingly.

Snow's face lights up and it's difficult not to feel a little lighter at his obvious pleasure.

"I'm listening."

"First, Duck has to agree to this." When he opens his mouth to argue, I hold up a hand. "That one is non-negotiable. If he doesn't agree, it doesn't happen."

"Okay. What else?"

"I get my own room. I don't care what theories you have about Duck and me, but I can assure you, you're way off base. My own room or it's no deal."

"You got it. And?"

"You don't tell Duck a word about what I just revealed to you. I don't want anyone to know."

"Do you think that's wise?"

"I don't give a shit if it is or not. Duck isn't to know my secret, got it?"

"Got it. Anything else?"

I pretend to think about it, but then shake my head. "No."

"That was easy," he quips. "Now, there are a few rules

you'll have to follow since you'll be on Satan's Legacy property."

"Wait, what?"

"Breathe, Grace. It's not as bad as you think. We all have our own homes at the compound. Duck lives with his..." He presses his lips together for a second before continuing. "Duck and Daisy are the only two people who live at his place. I can't say that you'll never see any of us there because we do drop in on each other from time to time. But otherwise, unless you choose to be around us, you don't have to be."

"Okay. What else?"

"You can come and go from the compound as you please. I'll make sure that you have clearance at the gate so you won't have any problems. But, you will have a security detail any time you leave."

"So I'll be a prisoner," I snip.

"No. Like I said, you can come and go as you please. But after Heather's—Sorry, the bitch whose blood runs through Daisy—accident, I'm not willing to take any chances. The club has enemies and with you staying there, they might make assumptions about your relationship. Which could make you a target." He rushes to add, "You can have friends at the compound though, as long as they submit to a background check. It will be your home, after all, at least for the foreseeable future."

"Remind me again why I should do this?" I agreed to help the father and daughter, not paint a bullseye on my back for MC enemies.

"Look, I'm probably being overly cautious, but I'd rather that than not cautious enough."

"That's fair, I guess." I might regret this, but... "Anything else?"

"One last thing. I need you to respect the fact that club business is just that, club business. Duck isn't permitted to talk to you about anything, so please don't push him for details. If it's something you need to know, you will."

"Come devote your life to a man and his daughter but remember your place." Sarcasm bleeds into the words. "You don't ask for much, do you?"

"I ask what I have to," he responds unapologetically. "It's my job to keep every single person in my club and on that compound safe. That now includes you."

"I guess I can respect that."

"Thank you."

"So, when will I be making the move?"

"As soon as we can get the doctor to discharge Daisy. He came by the room earlier today and said she can go as soon as she's up to a certain weight." Snow pauses for a beat. "But I'm hoping we can convince him to release her sooner since you're on board with her care."

"Yeah, that won't happen," I warn him.

"Everyone has a price."

"I know you like to throw the club's money around to get what you want, as evidenced by all the strings you've pulled here so far. But when it comes to this, Doc isn't gonna budge. And he shouldn't. If you're thinking that having me live with them will make a difference, think again. Because I won't agree to it until Daisy is officially, and appropriately, cleared medically."

Snow whistles. "Already playing mama bear. I like it."

"Make no mistake, Snow, I'm not Daisy's mama. She already has one of those, even if the woman doesn't give a damn about her."

"Okay. Whatever you say."

I roll my eyes. I want to argue, but it would be pointless.

I'm getting a crash course into how the man works, and when Snow sets his mind to something, he doesn't back down until it happens. And right now, he wants me to be Daisy's mom. I may have agreed to play along for a while, but only one little girl holds that maternal place in my heart and it's not Daisy.

Not yet.

The voice in my head clamors to be heard.

Not yet.

CHAPTER 12
DUCK
THREE WEEKS LATER...

Today is the day. Daisy has officially been discharged from the hospital and we're going home. It's exciting, yet I find myself with a permanent scowl.

"You better knock that shit off, D."

I look up from a sleeping Daisy to glare at Snow. Maybe I could genuinely enjoy all of this if he hadn't schemed behind my back to have Grace move in with me and then ordered my cooperation. He may be my best friend and think he's doing the right thing, but he's also my Prez and abusing his power by controlling my personal life.

"Knock what off?"

"All the brooding shit. You and your daughter are going home, man. Can't you just enjoy that?"

"Maybe I could, but we'll never know, will we?" I snap. "Because you had to go and move a woman in with us."

"You're right, I did." He smirks. "Your stubborn ass can thank me later."

I huff out a humorless laugh. "Not fucking likely."

Snow gasps and gently places his hands over Daisy's ears. "Language," he chastises mockingly.

I roll my eyes at him. "Stuff it. She's gonna grow up surrounded by rowdy bikers. She might as well fucking get used to it."

"Touché. But when her first word is motherfucker, don't come crying to me."

We banter back and forth for a few more minutes, only stopping when Grace enters the room. My gaze is drawn to her, much like it is every time she's near, and I'm surprised to see that she looks about as thrilled as I am about the prospect of her moving in.

The last three weeks have been tense, to say the least. Grace has held on to her snit about me leaving the hospital for club business, and I've held onto mine about... Shit, I don't even remember what it was about.

We haven't talked much either, which has made things between us very awkward. I guess we better get over that real goddamn quick.

"I've got all the paperwork," Grace says, holding up a folder for all of us to see.

Snow crosses the room to her and kisses her cheek. "Thanks, Grace."

The smile she beams at him has all of my muscles tensing with jealousy. Stupid, I know, but there you have it. I may not want her, but apparently, I don't want anyone else to get any part of her either.

Ridiculous.

"You're welcome."

Snow sneaks a glance at me, and his grin tells me that he's aware of my annoyance and he's getting a kick out of it. When he refocuses his attention on Grace, he oozes charm, knowing it'll rile me further.

"The guys will have your stuff to you by this evening. They're loading everything up now. I found someone to take over your lease. If and when you want to move off the compound, we'll help you find a new place."

"When, Snow, not if," she corrects him.

And that adds to my frustration. She hasn't even moved in yet and she's already planning her escape.

You don't want her there, remember?

Yeah, I fucking remember. But that doesn't mean I don't want her to want to be there.

I clear my throat. "We better get going. I don't want to catch rush hour traffic out of the city."

"Right," Grace says in agreement. "Her car seat is in my vehicle and all ready to go."

I stiffen. "Why is it in your car?"

It's Snow's turn to glare. "D, a car seat and a Harley don't mix. I figured you'd be itching to ride, so I had Grace put it in her car and we can transfer it to your truck when we get home."

Duh, idiot.

"Oh."

Daisy starts to cry, so I check her diaper, but it's dry. I bounce on my feet to try and calm her down, but that doesn't work. It isn't long before her cries become little baby screams and I panic because I don't know what to do.

Grace plucks her from my arms and holds her against her chest while rocking from side to side. She also puts a pacifier in her mouth, and Daisy calms within seconds. I may not want Grace moving in with me, but even I can't deny how handy it'll be having her around.

"She's just hungry. We should get her home so she can be fed," Grace says quietly.

"Then let's go."

Snow and I gather up all of our belongings and we all head to the parking lot. Grace shows me how to secure Daisy in her car seat. Once that's done, she slides into the driver's seat and starts the engine.

"Grace, you can follow me," Snow tells her through her open window. "Duck, you bring up the rear. That way you can keep an eye on your girls."

Grace groans at being lumped into that category, causing my hackles to rise. I mean, she could do worse than being my girl.

Stop! Enough.

It takes about forty-five minutes to reach the compound. The drive is agonizingly slow, but I know that's because Snow is being careful. We all park in front of my cabin, which is situated to the left of the clubhouse. Several of the brothers are standing on the front porch, as are Sami, Fallon, and Laney.

Magic comes down from the porch and helps Snow get everything inside, while I lift Daisy from her car seat and snuggle her to me. She's sleeping, so no one makes a big fuss over her, which I'm grateful for. It helps that they all visited numerous times at the hospital, rarely leaving me alone during visiting hours.

Snow comes back outside and walks straight to Grace, who I hadn't even noticed got out of her car and was staring at the welcome committee like she's facing a firing squad.

"Welcome home, Grace," he says as he steers her toward the porch.

Again, jealousy rears its ugly head, because I should be the one welcoming her home.

Instead, I'm holding on tightly to all the reasons I don't want her here and trying to ignore the reasons I do.

I stay behind my best friend and the woman who's making me question my sanity. I glance around the outside of my cabin, trying to see it from Grace's point of view. There are flower beds on either side of the porch steps, courtesy of Heather, but this time of year, nothing is blooming. There's also a porch swing and several chairs, all of which need a new paint job.

When I reach the door, I hesitate. Grace is already inside with Snow, who's giving her a tour of the place, but I can't quite bring myself to take another step.

A small hand comes to rest on my shoulder, and I look to my right to see Laney standing there, holding a sleeping Zoe.

"We cleaned out all her stuff," she says quietly, somehow knowing what's holding me back. "Most of it got donated to the shelters. Some of it was trashed, but we did leave a few things behind for you to do with what you want."

"Thanks," I mutter. "Appreciate it."

"Don't thank me. I wanted to burn it all, but my big brother wouldn't let me," she gripes.

I wink at her. "I'd have let you."

"That's what I told Snow. Stubborn man never listens." Laney moves her hand from my shoulder to brush it over Daisy's head of fine baby hair. "She's beautiful, Duck. Absolutely perfect."

"I just wish I knew what the fuck I was doing," I say. "She deserves a daddy who's as perfect as she is."

"Nah." Laney shakes her head. "She just needs a daddy who loves her and is willing to do anything for her. I'd say letting Grace move in here is a good start."

"Not like I had a choice."

"Maybe not. Look, all I'm saying is she's here to help.

Let her. Trust me, when Daisy's waking you up at all hours of the night, you're gonna be glad Grace is here."

"I hope you're right."

"I am." Laney pushes me through the door. "Now get in there and enjoy having your daughter home."

Once inside, my racing nerves settle slightly at seeing no trace of Heather, other than a small box pushed against the wall near the door. There are already pictures of Daisy on the walls, ones that were taken at the hospital. I focus on one in particular and recognize it as the one Grace took the first time I had skin-to-skin contact with my baby girl.

I press a kiss to the top of her tiny head and carry her toward the room that was meant to be her nursery. Because she was born so early, it never got comp—

"What the hell?" I mumble when I reach the door and see Snow and Grace inside.

"Whaddya think?" Snow asks, turning in a circle. "Pretty nice, right?"

I glance around the space, taking in everything. Two of the walls are painted pale pink while the other two have unicorn wallpaper. Daisy's crib is a bright white and there's a pink blanket draped over one end. Along one wall is a changing table, already stocked with all the necessities. And in one corner, there's an oversized leather recliner rather than the standard rocking chair that seems to be a fixture in every nursery everywhere.

"When did you do all this?" I ask, a lump forming in my throat.

Snow chuckles. "Dude, we've had plenty of time. Besides, Grace helped come up with a theme and color scheme. Once we had her ideas, Sami, Fallon, and Laney did all the shopping while the brothers did all the heavy lifting."

"You helped?" I ask Grace.

She lowers her head for a moment and takes a deep breath. When her eyes meet mine, she nods.

"It's incredible," I say, and I mean it. "Thank you."

"You're welcome."

"Hey, what about me?" Snow grumbles. "We did all the hard work."

"Yeah, yeah. Thanks."

Snow closes the distance between us and bends to kiss Daisy on the top of her head. "Sweet, sweet Daisy. Your dad is a dick."

"And keeping in line with that reputation, her dad is now kicking you out." I laugh at the flat look he gives me. "Seriously, go. I wanna get settled in."

Snow turns to Grace. "You okay if I leave?"

My body goes rigid. "I'm not gonna fucking hurt her. Jesus."

"Grace?" Snow prods.

"I'm fine," she tells him, completely ignoring me. "If I can't handle him, I've got your number."

"Okay. The guys should be here in an hour or two with your stuff. Whatever you don't want here, just let them know and they'll get it into storage for you."

"Thanks, Snow."

"Anytime." Snow starts out of the room but pauses to look over his shoulder at me. "Behave."

Just as the front door closes, signaling that he's really left, Daisy starts crying.

"I'll go fix her a bottle," Grace says on her way out of the room.

My mind screams at me to follow her, but I don't. Instead, I carry a crying Daisy around the room, pointing out all of the things that are all hers. It doesn't calm her one bit, but the simple activity does wonders for me.

That is until my phone vibrates in my pocket and I look at the screen. My blood boils at the text, rage begging to be released.

Unknown number: Not even a little surprised you've moved another bitch in. You always were a player. Give the brat a hug for me.

What the ever-loving fuck?!

CHAPTER 13

GRACE

"I gotta go."

I look up from a sleeping Daisy at the man standing in the doorway. At the hospital, Duck was in my territory, and it was easy to put distance between us if he pissed me off. But now I'm in his, and there's nowhere for me to go.

"Seriously?" I whisper as I turn on the baby monitor and tiptoe out of the room. "You just got her home and now you're leaving?"

For a very brief moment, guilt flickers in his gaze. But he masks it quickly with his usual look of indifference.

"Just because I'm a father now doesn't mean the rest of my life stops. I've got church, and it's mandatory."

"What the hell kinda church is mandatory?"

"The kind that has nothing to do with religion and everything to do with this cut I wear," he snaps as he smacks the leather on his chest.

"So once again, you're putting the club before Daisy."

I know I sound judgmental, but it's impossible not to. His priorities seem to be all jacked up.

"This club is what will keep clothes on her back, formula in her bottles, and this roof over her head." Duck's face is red, and he's practically vibrating with frustration. "Oh, and this club is what's putting money into your bank account for being here."

Properly put in my place, for now, I quit arguing. "Look, I'm sorry, okay? I'm tired and in a home that doesn't belong to me with a man who doesn't like me. Forgive me if I'm a little cranky."

Duck's eyes narrow and he frowns. "I never said I didn't like you."

I snort at that. "You didn't have to."

Duck grabs my arm and practically drags me down the hallway into the living room. "Sit down," he commands, pointing at the couch. When I do as I'm told, he begins to pace. "It's not that I don't like you, Grace. It's just..." He shoves a hand through his hair. "The last time I was in this house was with my pregnant fiancée and life was great." He stops in front of me and locks eyes with mine. "Then someone hit the truck she was driving, and my baby was born by emergency c-section. To top it off, the bitch left the hospital with the help of another man and hasn't once checked on her preemie newborn. And now I'm back here with no idea how my life got so fucked up, and I have a little girl who is depending on me to be strong for her and you, who I have no goddamn clue what to do with. I shouldn't like you; I shouldn't think about you nonstop when there are a million other things I should be worrying about. But I can't seem to stop myself. It's not you I don't like, Grace. It's me."

Wow, okay. That's a lot. I knew Daisy's mother had taken off. I'd seen her chart where she left the hospital AMA, against medical advice. I witnessed the aftermath when Duck tore her room apart, decimating it until it was unrecognizable. But I didn't know all the details. I'm not sure if they help or not, but I'm glad he told me.

Before I can respond, Duck is striding toward the door. He pauses with his hand on the doorknob. He doesn't look back, simply stares straight ahead at the wall.

"This is your home, Grace. At least for now. Go ahead and unpack. You can put stuff wherever you want. I know you think I'm an asshole and you're not wrong, but I *do* want you to be comfortable. I'll be back in a few hours."

He quietly closes the door behind him, and the lock engages before his footsteps pound on the porch as he walks away.

After he's gone, I decide to make use of my time and head to my new bedroom to unpack like he said I should. I set the baby monitor on the dresser the brothers brought from my apartment. The only furniture I decided to keep here was my bedroom set. Duck has everything else and there's no point in stuffing his cabin full of duplicate things.

I pull my cell phone out of my pocket and open up my music app. I hit play when I find my favorite southern rock playlist, but I make sure to keep the volume low enough so as not to wake Daisy. Then I go about putting my clothes away.

Once I finish that, I find the box labeled bathroom and move to the en suite. I'd gotten a good look at it earlier, when Snow showed me around, but I'm still a little in awe of how chic it is. There's a large clawfoot tub and a walk-in shower. The color scheme is dark gray with white and silver accents. Hell, there's even a small chandelier hanging from the ceiling. It looks like it was lifted out of a magazine and dropped into place, just for me.

Snow told me that he and a few of the others added the

bathroom once they knew I was moving in and made sure to point out that it had been at Duck's request. He also explained that the walk-in closet was an upgrade Duck asked for as well.

That still flabbergasts me. For someone who doesn't want me here, he sure went to a lot of trouble to make sure I was comfortable. Except... that's not entirely true, according to the man himself, if his earlier statements are to be believed. It's not that he doesn't want me here, it's more that he has no clue what to do with me now that I *am* here.

Duck is an enigma full of so many layers, I'm not sure that I'll ever truly understand him. But the more time I spend with him and the more layers he carefully peels away for me to see, the more I find I really want to try. Despite all the twisted-up emotions being in his presence evokes.

My music shifts to 'It's Raining Men', the ringtone Vince insisted I have for him, and I can't help but smile.

"Hey, Vince," I say when I answer.

"Hey chicky, how's it going?"

I sit on the edge of my bed and sigh. "I don't even know how to answer that."

"That bad?"

"No, not bad exactly. Just... weird, I guess."

"Weird can be good, ya know?"

I outright laugh at that. "It's not kinky weird so get your mind outta the gutter."

"Ah, well. Maybe someday."

"I think I might be living vicariously through you until I'm well into my eighties," I tease, although there might be some truth to that if things keep going the way they are.

"Nope, not gonna happen. You, Grace Knowles, are

going to get the fairytale you deserve. And something tells me it will involve lots of leather and denim."

Choosing to ignore that statement, I change the subject. "Hey, I want you to see something. Gonna put you on FaceTime."

"Ugh, fine," he grumbles.

Once we're connected, I walk back to the bathroom and turn the camera around. Vince gasps.

"Holy shit, that's gorgeous."

"Isn't it?" I giggle.

"I have to say, I did not see that as part of a house a biker owns."

I flip the camera back around so I can see him. "Me either," I say and pull my lip between my teeth.

"Okay, what? There's more to this than a surprising bathroom."

"That bathroom was added just for me," I confide.

"Come again?"

"You heard me. Duck asked the club to add a bathroom for me, as well as make the closet a walk-in. I mean, who does that?"

"None of the men I date, that's for sure."

"That's just it, Vince. Duck and I aren't dating. Half the time we can't even be in the same room together."

"Grace, a man doesn't do shit like that if he doesn't like the person he's doing it for."

"He says he doesn't know what to do with me. That he doesn't like himself because he likes me."

"Interesting."

I snort. "Frustrating and confusing is more like it."

"Yeah, that too."

"What do I do, Vince?"

"You take it a day at a time, chicky. If this all ends and

you move out, fine. You'll land on your feet. But my advice is to see where it goes and stop fighting whatever the fuck it is between you too."

"I'm pretty sure he isn't looking for a relationship."

"And according to you, you aren't either."

"True."

"But there's nothing that says you two can't be friends, right?"

"Well, no."

"Then start there."

Daisy's wailing cry pierces the air at the same time chaos descends around Vince.

"Looks like we both gotta go," I say, not wanting to end the conversation.

"Probably another OD on my end. There have been four already today."

"I'm sorry. Suddenly, facing a dirty diaper doesn't seem so bad."

"Eww. I'll leave the puke and shit to you." Vince glances over his shoulder at the gurney being wheeled through the ER to a bay. "I'll call you in a few days, chicky."

And with that, the phone goes blank, and my music starts back up. I toss the cell onto my bed and race to the nursery, where Daisy is squirming around in her crib.

"Hey, baby," I coo as I scoop her into my arms. "What seems to be the problem?"

I change her diaper and feed her a bottle, but nothing works to calm her down. I try rocking her back and forth, cuddling her in the recliner, and walking through the house humming. Nothing fucking works.

There's one more thing I can try, but I'm hesitant. I have no idea when Duck will be back, and I don't want to get caught in a compromising position. Daisy's shrieking intensifies.

Fuck it.

I place her in her crib while I pull my shirt over my head. I leave my bra on, not comfortable being completely bare, and pick Daisy back up for some skin-to-skin contact. I take the little pink blanket draped over her crib and cover myself before settling in the recliner.

It takes a few minutes, but Daisy quiets and falls asleep. I debate about getting up and putting her in her crib but decide against it. It feels good to have her against me, relying on me for her comfort. Probably too good considering I'm not her mother.

I promise myself I'll only sit here for a little while. But when I close my eyes, exhaustion takes over and I'm out.

CHAPTER 14
DUCK

"Welcome back brother."

Dip slaps me on the back as he moves into the meeting room.

"It's good to be back."

And it is. I've missed the clubhouse and everything that comes along with it. I was kept in the loop while at the hospital with Daisy, but I still felt like I was on the outside looking in. Well, I'm back and ready to reclaim my seat as VP and fuck some shit up.

Magic races through the door at the last minute and practically dives into his seat.

"You were this close to being late," I tell him as I hold my thumb and pointer finger a fraction of an inch apart.

"Blame it on Zoe." He grins. "It was her tiny hands refusing to let me leave."

"That's no excuse," I remind him.

"Yeah, it is. You just wait, D. You'll be scrambling in here just like me before you know it. And all because of a little girl who has you wrapped around her finger."

"I'd pay to see that," Dip teases.

"When will tickets go on sale?" Toga taunts.

"Okay, that's enough," Snow says, rising from his chair at the head of the table. "You can all go back to giving Duck a hard time after we deal with business first."

"You heard the man," I bellow, and then begin church. "What the patch binds together, let no force tear apart. Satan's Legacy now and forever."

"First of all, I want to start off by congratulating Duck again on the birth of his daughter." Cheers erupt around the table and Snow holds up a hand to shush them all. "Make sure you stop by and meet Grace, the nurse that's staying with Duck and Daisy for a while to help out. She's under our protection and one of our own for now. I expect you to treat her as such."

"In other words, don't go treating her like some club whore. She's not up for grabs," I tack on.

"Aw, come on," Spark, our treasurer whines. "It's been a while since we've had fresh pussy around here."

I see red. Snow's hands grab at my cut when I try to launch myself over the table at Spark. My prez shoves me down into my chair and keeps a grip on my shoulder to make sure I don't try anything again.

"So, it's like that?" Spark asks.

"Spark, if you wanna dip your wick and club sluts ain't doin' it for ya, go to a fucking bar," Snow seethes. "I don't give a good goddamn if it's like that with Duck or not. Grace is off limits, got it?"

Spark holds his hands up in surrender. "Got it, Prez."

Snow points his finger at each brother around the table. "That goes for everyone else too."

Murmurs of agreement surround me, yet it's not enough. I rise from my chair again, giving Snow a look to let him know I'm not going to do anything stupid. He removes his hand and gives a curt nod.

"Grace is mine," I say evenly. I have no idea what's driving me to claim her, other than the idea of anyone touching her ignites a fire in my soul that I thought was long snuffed out. "Anyone goes near her with anything other than friendship in mind, and you'll answer to me. Touch her and I'll break your fingers. Hurt her and I'll snap your neck. Understood?"

"We hear ya, bro," Dip says. "If we wanna fuck, find another bitch."

"Exactly."

"Now that we've successfully measured our peckers, let's return to business," Snow says and shifts his stare to Spark. "Any financial updates?"

"Nothing good, Prez. All payments from places we provide security are coming in on time. Fallon's non-profit, Source of Love, is raking in donations so that's self-sufficient. But we're moving closer and closer to the red with the drug runs. This fucking Dracula is killing our profits."

"How are we not any closer to figuring out who the hell he is?" I ask.

"Because no one is talking," Dip snaps. "All of our contacts have quit feeding us information. Somehow, he got to them. Not sure if he paid them or just bribed them with an endless supply of red pills."

"My money's on the pills," Snow interjects. "We pay our people well and treat our contacts like they matter."

"We're missing something," I say as I shove a hand through my hair. "I don't know what, but my gut tells me that when we figure out what it is, everything else will click into place."

"Any thoughts on how to figure it the fuck out?" Snow asks.

"Actually, yeah." I shift my gaze to Magic. "I think you should round up a few of our contacts and bring 'em back to the shed. They know more than they're saying. Get 'em to divulge their secrets."

"And if they don't talk?" Toga pipes in.

"Then kill 'em." I shrug. "They've already proven that they aren't loyal by keeping their mouths shut. That can't go unpunished."

"All those in favor of torturing contacts, say 'aye'."

And the 'ayes' have it.

"I'm gonna take it a step further." Snow leans forward, flattening his palms on the table. "I think we should do the same with a few of our runners. The more people we interrogate, the better chance we have of walking away with useful information."

"I'm in," Magic says as he cracks his knuckles.

Another vote is taken and again, the 'ayes' have it.

"We'll meet back up in a few days about that," Snow states. "Now, any updates on Heather's whereabouts?"

"I talked with Connie during my shift at the shelter last night and she still hasn't heard from her," Carnie, our club doc, says.

"Has she shown up at the shelter at all since Daisy was born?" I ask.

"No." Toga shakes his head. "Connie received a letter in the mail the following day saying that Heather wouldn't be returning to work. Also had the same shit telling Connie not to look for her. No return address."

"It came in the mail? Like snail mail?"

Toga nods.

"How is that possible?" I counter. "Heather didn't know she was going to be having Daisy or that she was—"

I press my lips together as the realization hits. Heather knew all along that she was leaving. That's the only thing that makes sense now that I know she mailed a letter to Connie. She knew exactly what was gonna happen. She planned the whole thing.

... because he's a ghost.

Bubba's words in the shed come back to haunt me. What if 'he' is actually a 'she'? And what if that 'she' is Heather?

"Son of a bitch!" I roar. "She's behind it all."

"Who's behind what?" Dip asks for clarification.

"Heather," I bark. "She set up the entire fucking accident."

Rage unlike anything I've ever felt curls around me and sinks into my pores. My body vibrates from the intensity and if that bitch were in front of me right now, I have no doubt I'd forget that a man shouldn't hit a woman.

Wouldn't have to hit her to kill her.

"But why?" Snow asks. "Why would she do that? And when she was pregnant no less."

"Evil doesn't need a reason," I snarl. "And that's exactly what she is. Pure fucking evil. I'm gonna go out on a limb and say she had no intention of Daisy surviving that accident."

How can a mother do that to her own child? I may not be the slightest bit confident in my ability to be a good father to Daisy, but to hurt her? To end her life before it even began? That's inconceivable to me. I loved her the moment I laid eyes on her, despite how I acted.

Not to mention, her botched attempt at ending the

pregnancy put Daisy in the NICU, fighting for her life while hooked up to machines and shit.

"I don't care what it takes, we find her, and we make her pay."

"All in favor?"

'Ayes' echo around the table.

"I got a text message from an unknown number earlier today. I think it was Heather. Spark, can you see if you can trace it?" I ask.

"Sure thing. Before you head back to your place, let me see it and I'll take it from there."

"Thanks, bro."

"Anytime. If you're right, and Heather planned that accident, I want her to suffer as much as you do."

"We all do," Snow says as he grips my shoulder in support. "She'll fucking pay dearly for this. I promise you that."

We spend the next twenty minutes plotting and planning ways to track Heather down and after church is adjourned, I stick around for another ten while Spark downloads data from my phone. The entire time, I'm antsy. I want to go home and see Daisy with my own eyes, remind myself that she's alive and healthy.

I walk out one of the side doors of the clubhouse and practically run the few yards to my cabin. When I step inside, I hear music playing from one of the bedrooms, so I stroll down the hallway to find the source.

Grace's bedroom door is open and on her bed is her cell phone. Lynyrd Skynyrd's 'Gimme Back my Bullets' flows from the device, and I'm surprised that our tastes in music are so in sync.

I make my way to the nursery, assuming that's where both of them are. The door is ajar, but the room is dark. I creep inside, careful not to make a sound in case Daisy is sleeping and lose my breath at the moonlit sight before me.

Grace is kicked back on the recliner and Daisy is fast asleep on her chest. Her almost naked chest. Her shirt is draped over the arm of the recliner, and it looks like she tried to cover up with one of the small pink blankets, but it has slipped down to rest near her waist. Daisy's tiny hand is gripping the edge of a white cotton bra, almost exposing Grace's nipple.

The entire scene shifts something in my heart, as well as in my pants.

CHAPTER 15
GRACE

My body aches, so I shift in my bed, but my eyes fly open when it's leather I feel against my skin and not the cotton-poly blend of sheets. For a moment, I forget where I am, but when my eyes land on a crib, it hits me that I'm in Daisy's nursery.

Daisy!

I must have fallen asleep with her on my chest, but she's not there now. I shoot to my feet and cross to the crib, expecting to see her there, but it's empty. It's dark out, so I must not have slept that long, but where the hell is Daisy?

I race out of the nursery and down the hall but slide to a halt when my sock covered feet hit the hardwood floor of the living room. Duck is sitting on the couch, and he's feeding Daisy a bottle. The television is tuned into some infomercial about cookware and the entire scene is very... domestic.

Duck must sense I'm here, or he heard me come barreling down the hall, because he twists his head around to look at me. I expect him to say something, but instead, he remains quiet. In the faint light that the television casts over the room, I see his nostrils flare and his biceps flex.

He clears his throat. "You're awake."

Unable to speak, I nod.

"You, uh, might want to put a shirt on," he says weakly.

I glance down at myself only to be reminded that I had taken my shirt off before settling into the recliner with Daisy. My simple bra does nothing to cover the evidence of how seeing him affects me. I cross my arms over my pebbled nipples.

Without a word, I turn on my heel and head to my room to put a shirt on. I settle on a tee and hoodie, but I also take my bra off. It's the middle of the night and bras weren't made to wear twenty-four-seven.

By the time I return to the living room, Duck has finished feeding Daisy. The empty bottle is sitting on the coffee table and he's pacing while he tries to burp her. I take the few seconds his back is turned to me and admire the view.

A pair of low-slung sweats rest at his hips and there's no hint of boxers, or anything for that matter, beneath. He's not wearing a shirt and his feet are bare. My stomach does a little flip-flop, and I have to clench my thighs together and remind my inner hussy that we're not here to get laid. We're here to do a job.

"Looks like that should be illegal," I mumble to myself.

"What?" Duck asks when he's facing me.

"What? Huh?" I frantically shake my head. "Nothing." I move to the couch and sit down, hugging a pillow to my chest. "So, how'd business go?"

At that, Duck's face morphs from contentment to fury. "Fine."

"Your words say one thing but your face..." I wave a circle in the air. "It says something else entirely."

"I can't talk about it," he grates out.

I flash back to my conversation with Snow. He made it very clear that I can't push Duck to talk about anything that's club business. I want to ask more questions, dig for information so Duck can unburden himself, but I said I wouldn't.

I shrug as if it's no big deal. "Okay."

Duck narrows his eyes at me in disbelief. "Okay? Just like that?"

"Yep. Just like that."

He continues pacing for a moment before speaking. "Thank you."

"For what?"

"For not pushing. For understanding that I can't talk about it."

"Well, you've made it perfectly clear that club business is not my business. It's pointless to push when your response will always be the same."

"You know it's not personal, yeah?"

As easy as it would be to make it personal, I do get what he's saying. I'm not the only person who doesn't get to know about a lot of things pertaining to Satan's Legacy. Even though I don't like it, I get it.

"I know."

Duck breathes a sigh of relief and I find myself happy to have given him that sense of peace, even if it is only for a moment.

"I'm gonna go put Daisy in her crib. I'll be right back."

When I'm alone, I let my mind wander. I don't know the precise moment I decided to make the most of the time I have here, but it seems I have. Whether it was Vince's encouragement, my attraction to Duck, or the father/daughter duo themselves, it doesn't matter. I can continue to be miserable, or I can use this opportunity for what it is: a chance for me to live outside of work and depression.

I'm choosing the latter.

"Are you hungry?" Duck asks from the kitchen. I'd been so wrapped up in my thoughts I didn't even realize he came back out.

"I could eat."

"Do you like scrambled eggs?"

"Yes."

I start to stand up, but Duck stops me. "Stay there and relax. I'm not the best cook, but I can handle eggs." He nods at the television. "There's Netflix on there. Why don't you see if there's anything to watch?"

"Okay." I lean forward and grab the remote. "What are you in the mood for?"

"You pick."

Scrolling through the options, I settle on a true crime documentary. Minutes later, Duck is carrying two plates piled high with fluffy eggs, two forks, and a bottle of ketchup.

"I added some cheese to them," he says as he hands me a plate and fork. "I hope that's okay."

"Mmm, that's perfect."

Duck's shoulders relax and he sits on the opposite end of the couch. He squeezes so much ketchup onto his plate that the eggs are barely visible. I scrunch up my nose at him.

"What?"

"You might as well forget the eggs and just squeeze ketchup straight into your mouth."

He laughs at that, and the sound wraps around me like a thick blanket. I like it when he laughs... probably too much.

"Let me guess, not a ketchup fan?" He quirks a brow.

"I like it just fine. As a condiment, not a meal."

"Eat," he orders, pointing his fork at me. I add a little ketchup to my plate to dip my eggs in and then set the bottle down on the coffee table. "So, what're we watchin'?"

"A documentary about Ted Bundy."

"Seriously? You like that shit?"

"Who doesn't?"

His eyes become almost vacant, but it passes so quickly, I tell myself I imagined it. "A lot of people."

"Are you one of those people?" I ask, hoping like hell he isn't.

"No. I love anything true crime."

I pretend to be relieved. "Oh thank God. For a minute there I thought I was gonna have to cancel my subscription to our friendship."

Duck chuckles as he snatches the remote up off the cushion between us and hits play. We both focus on eating and the documentary.

Once I've polished off my eggs, I curl up on the couch, careful not to touch Duck. He keeps his eyes on the television but grabs my ankles and stretches my legs to rest in his lap. At first, I stiffen, confused by the action, but it isn't long before I'm relaxing. Being like this, with him, feels natural.

And a little scary.

I must fall asleep because the next thing I know, I'm being lifted from the couch and cradled against Duck's bare chest. I burrow in deeper and inhale the scent of him, completely content in his arms.

"Keep that up and you won't be sleeping alone tonight," he rasps against my head.

"Don't ruin the moment," I whisper.

Duck carries me into my room and lays me on the bed. He pulls the covers up and places a kiss on my forehead.

"Get some sleep, Grace."

I listen as he crosses the room and just before he steps through the doorway, I roll over.

"Duck?"

He glances over his shoulder. "Yeah, Grace?"

"You really don't hate me, do you?"

His smile is sad.

"No, Grace, I really don't."

CHAPTER 16
DUCK

What. The. Fuck?

Back in my room, I strip out of my sweats, set my cell on my nightstand, and crawl into bed, all the while doing my damndest to ignore my rock-hard cock. Rigid is apparently the new status quo for my dick when it comes to Grace. Other than when I was feeding Daisy, he's been at attention.

There's no denying I'm attracted to Grace. More than attracted. Her rich, chocolate brown hair reaches just past her shoulders, and at the hospital, she usually wore it up in a messy bun. She has these piercing green eyes that darken when she's angry and lighten when she laughs. No more than five foot two, she has curves for days and tits I want to bury my face in. A plain white bra never looked so sexy.

Grace's beauty is understated but no less tempting than Aphrodite herself.

It's no secret that, before Heather, I was the resident player. But different nameless women every night got old, and I wanted what my brothers had. I wanted love. I thought I had it, but obviously, I was wrong. As bitter and angry as I am at Heather, I'd be lying if I said I'd change any of it because now I have Daisy.

And Grace.

I groan at that thought. I don't *have* Grace. She's being paid to be here. But I think I might want her. Definitely to fuck, and if I'm being honest, probably for more than that.

I roll over and punch my pillow to try and get comfortable. I'm not convinced I'll actually get any sleep, not with thoughts of Grace running through my head, but I can pretend to try.

Tossing and turning is how I spend the rest of the night until the sun streams through the blinds. I kick the sheet off and go about my morning routine. Piss, shower, dress, coffee. I'm just finishing my first cup when Daisy starts crying.

I half expect to run into Grace in the hall, but I don't. It takes me far too long to change Daisy's diaper. Little girl sure knows how to shit a mess. I dress her in a clean onesie and carry her out to the kitchen to get her a bottle but get sidetracked when there's a knock at the door.

Sensing the detour from her formula, Daisy's crying intensifies.

"I know. Daddy's gonna feed you."

I unlock and open the door and before he's even over the threshold, Snow is plucking Daisy from my arms and walking circles around the room to try and calm her. And dammit, it works.

"Good morning to you too asshole," I mutter.

"Get used to it, D." Snow chuckles. "Any visitors you get from now on will be here to see this precious little nugget and not your ugly mug."

I've known Snow for years and seen him around plenty of kids, but I'll never get used to my best friend using baby talk.

"Well, don't just stand there," he grumbles. "Fix this little lady a bottle. She's hungry."

You can't kill him because he's holding your daughter.

While I go about exactly what I was planning on doing, *without his order to do so*, I listen to him carry on a one-sided conversation with Daisy. I find myself smiling when he dives into a speech about how she can't date until she's thirty and how, if any boy ever makes her cry, her daddy and uncles will 'take care of them' for her.

"You know she doesn't understand a word you're saying, right?"

Snow's expression of shock has me grinning. "Of course she does."

"Whatever helps you sleep at night."

"Speaking of sleep, it looks like you haven't gotten any in weeks."

"Sleeping in a hospital will do that to ya."

"And I suppose sleeping just down the hall from a certain someone doesn't factor in?"

"What doesn't factor into what?"

Both Snow and I whip our heads to stare at Grace, who looks fuckably adorable with her hair and clothes rumpled from sleep.

"Oh, uh—"

"Club business," Snow says when he realizes I'm struggling.

Grace darts her eyes back and forth between us, and I hold my breath and cross my fingers that she believes his lie. Finally, she shrugs.

"Okay." She walks to Snow and holds her arms out. "Give her to me, and I'll feed her."

"I can feed her," I tell her, but she's shaking her head.

"I got her. You two talk." Grace grabs the bottle out of my hands and moves to sit on the couch. "Pretend I'm not here."

Snow gives me a look that says 'is she for real' and I shrug before pouring coffee for both of us. He joins me at the kitchen table, and we make sure to keep our voices low.

"Any more texts from Heather?" he asks.

"No." I pull my cell from my cut and glance at it just to be sure. "I take it Spark hasn't traced the number yet."

"No, sorry." Snow sips on his coffee. "We'll keep at it. I wanted to talk to you real quick about Dracula."

"What about him?"

"I know we provide security for the shelters and we're already on track to bring in contacts and runners for interrogation." He glances over his shoulder to make sure Grace isn't listening. Satisfied that she isn't, he continues. "But I want to do more than that. I was thinking that maybe we could get some of the people who utilize the shelters to talk. The homeless population is just as affected by the fucker as anyone else. We've seen enough ODs to prove it."

"That's not a bad idea. Do you really think they'll talk?"

"I don't know, but it's worth a shot."

"You gonna bring it to a vote?"

Snow nods. "In a few days. I wanna give enough time to see if we get anything from the interrogations first." His eyes light up. "Speaking of, Magic has two of our contacts in the shed. I know you've got a lot of shit to work out and figured you'd want to join him."

"Damn straight I do. Let me get things situated here first. Should be there within the hour."

Snow slaps a hand on the table. "Sounds good, brother. Let me know what you guys find out."

"Will do."

Snow stands and walks to the front door. "Grace, I hope you don't mind, but Sami and the other ladies are planning on stopping by later today."

"Of course, I don't mind." She looks at me. "Unless you aren't okay with it."

"I don't have a problem with it at all."

"Good," Snow says. "I'll tell Sami to give you an hour or two to get Daisy settled, otherwise they'll descend on you like a hoard of vultures within two minutes of me giving them the green light."

Once Snow is gone, I move to the couch. "Here, let me finish up with her while you have some coffee."

Grace hands me my daughter, but I don't miss the slight hesitation to give her up. I watch as Grace goes about filling a mug and then searches for something to eat, settling on a strawberry pop tart.

I find myself staring at the way her lips wrap around the pastry every time she takes a bite, and the way her eyes practically roll back in her head as she enjoys its sugary goodness. Quickly, I push to my feet and turn toward the hall.

"I'm gonna go deal with diaper duty. I have to leave in about forty-five minutes, so if you want a shower or anything, you've got some uninterrupted time now."

"Are you sure?" Grace bites her lower lip. "I mean, I'm here to help with Daisy, not to have a girls' day."

"Yeah, you're here to help, but like I said before, this is your home now. When Snow asked you to do this, it wasn't his intention for you not to have a life."

"Okay, well, if you're sure."

"I'm sure. Now go."

Grace rinses her mug in the sink and then rushes to her room. I, on the other hand, get Daisy settled and continue to ignore the bulge in my jeans.

CHAPTER 17

GRACE

When Snow told me that Sami and the others would be coming over, I was nervous. I've spent time with all of them, at the hospital, but that was different. That was at work. But now that they're here, I find my nerves were for nothing.

"Wait until she starts walking!" Sami laughs, but quickly sobers and gives me an apologetic look. "Sorry, Grace. I keep forgetting that you won't always be here."

I force a smile. "No worries."

"I, for one, am crossing all my fingers and toes that you never leave," Laney says and widens her eyes. "I mean, can you picture Duck with Daisy all by himself?" She mock shudders.

"He's actually really good with her," I say, feeling the need to defend him. "It was iffy in the beginning, and I know he's afraid he'll do something wrong, but he shouldn't be."

"Duck?" Sami asks for clarification. "Our Duck? He's good with her?" I must not hide my frustration very well because she quickly adds, "I'm just kidding. We all are."

"Oh."

"Look, Duck has always sort of been the class clown. It's hard to picture him in the single father role. I mean, he was thrilled when he found out Heather was pregnant. We all were. But then she left and, well, you saw what happened. He's not exactly the picture of fatherly bliss." Sami groans. "Shit. You should just duct tape my mouth shut because I'm always saying the wrong thing around you."

"It's fine, really. It isn't as if I didn't know about her or that Daisy has a mother somewhere." But... "What was she like?"

"Heather?"

"Yeah."

"She's a fucking bitch who deserves to have her throat slit," Laney snaps. We all stare at her like she's got a horn sticking out of her head. "What?" She shrugs. "It's true. After what she did, I'd pay money to watch our men punish her."

I don't correct her 'our men' comment. Duck isn't my man.

"What did she do?" I ask. I know she left, but the way she said it makes me think there's a lot more to that story.

"Yeah," Fallon says. "What do you know that we don't?"

Laney's shoulders sag. "Dammit, Magic is gonna kill me." She seems to think about it for a minute and then says, "I'll tell you what I know, but you can't say a word."

"Who the fuck are we gonna tell?" Fallon asks.

Laney chuckles. "Girl, all Toga has to do to get you to spill your secrets is lick your clit and make you squirm."

"And how's that any different with you and Magic?"

"It's not." Laney grins. "How do you think I know as much as I do? A little dick sucking, and he can't keep his mouth shut."

"Oh my God," Sami groans. "If Snow knew that, he'd shit."

"Bullshit," Laney counters with a laugh. "You can't honestly sit there and tell me you don't have your ways of getting information from my brother."

Sami tilts her head to the side. "Well, there is this one thing I do with my tongue and his—"

"Nope, no, do *not* finish that sentence," Laney instructs. "I don't need to know."

The look of horror on Laney's face has us all rolling with laughter. I laugh so hard, tears start running down my cheeks. I can't remember the last time I let go like this.

Sami is the first to sober up and she slaps her hands on the table to get our attention. Once she has it, she stares at Laney.

"Spill," she demands. "What do you know?"

Laney heaves a sigh. "Apparently, the guys think Heather planned the accident."

"You've gotta be fucking kidding me," Fallon snaps.

"Nope. But it gets worse. I guess Duck's working theory is that she did all this to end the pregnancy."

Outraged, I shoot to my feet. "What kind of person does that? What kind of woman tries to kill her own baby? Why would she do that? I can't..." I pause and take in the wide-eyed shock on each of their faces. "What?"

"You seem pretty passionate about this," Fallon comments.

"I am because..." I almost tell them my secret. Almost. It wouldn't surprise me one bit if they already knew, seeing as how Snow and the other brothers apparently suck at keeping information to themselves. "It's just sad, that's all."

Fallon eyes me suspiciously but doesn't comment on

whatever it is she's thinking. Maybe she senses that I'm holding something back, but I can't worry about that now.

"It's criminal is what it is," Sami snaps. "I can't imagine what made her do it."

"None of us can," Laney agrees. "Whatever the reason, she's not gonna get away with it, that's for sure."

Now that Laney's divulged the information, the mood shifts. The air thickens around us and all the fun we were having dissipates under the weight of what Heather did.

A phone beeps and we all pull our devices out to see whose it was.

"It's me," Laney says. "The babysitter has to leave, so I need to get back to Zoe and Shiloh."

"Yeah, I should probably head home and scrounge up some dinner for Snow and Lennox," Sami says.

"I'm gonna go home and fuck my husband. All that talk about licking clits and dicks has me horny," Fallon adds.

I see them all out and as I'm closing the door, Daisy wakes from her nap. The next several hours pass in a frenzy of feedings, diaper changes, napping, and unpacking more of my belongings.

Just as I'm about to start another documentary on Netflix, Duck comes through the front door. I turn to tell him that I left him a plate of food in the microwave, but no words come out when I see the state he's in.

Duck's shirt is covered in blood and there's a large hole ripped in it right over his pec. His cut looks spotless, but then again, it always does. His knuckles are scraped and bloody and a bruise is forming on his cheek.

I rush to him, but he holds a hand up to stop me.

"Don't."

I lock eyes with him. "You're hurt."

"Trust me, I'm a far sight better than the other guys."

I fall back a step. Other guys? Does he mean his Satan's Legacy brothers or someone else, someone who fucked up and paid the ultimate price? I don't know why the thought bothers me. I've seen that show on television about motorcycle clubs. I know violence comes with the territory but seeing the evidence of it in person is so much different than seeing it acted out.

"I'm gonna shower and then spend some time with my daughter," Duck says before walking past me toward his room.

I want to call him back, to ask the dozens of questions running through my mind, but I don't. Because I know his response will be 'club business'.

Now, more than ever, I wish I could use the ways of the ol' ladies to extract his secrets.

CHAPTER 18
DUCK

It's been less than twenty-four hours since Magic and I eliminated the contacts who were brought to the shed. Turns out, they were being paid in pills to stop giving us information. It didn't work out so well for either of them because they both paid Satan's Legacy with their lives.

But not all hope was lost because we're back at it again. Same shit, different day.

My knuckles are raw, and my muscles burn with every punch I throw. Kenny and Phil, two of our drug runners, are tied to chairs in front of me. They seem to be suffering from a case of amnesia, so my pain won't stop until they start remembering shit.

"Maybe they really don't know anything," Magic comments from his position in the corner of the shed.

Without taking my eyes off of them, I snarl, "They're drug runners who've shit on us by pushing someone else's product. They know something." I smirk. "Don't ya boys?"

"I don't know nothin'," Kenny, the smaller of the two, whines.

I stride over to Magic and hold out my hand for the baggie he took off of the punk when they first arrived. Snatching it from his hand, I storm back and shove it in Kenny's face.

"Then what the fuck are these red pills?" The scent of urine makes its way into my nostrils. I glance down and shake my head. "Did you seriously just piss yourself?"

Kenny swings his head from side to side in a feverish attempt to answer me but the puddle forming under him reveals his lie.

Phil, the more hardened criminal of the two, is staring at Kenny, rolling his eyes like he can't believe the pussy is acting so weak. Problem is, I haven't focused on Phil yet, so he should probably reserve his judgment.

"Where did you get these?" I ask Kenny again.

He says nothing, so I bring my knife up to just below his ear.

"Answer me!" I roar as I push the tip of the blade through his skin.

"I, uh, I..." His scared eyes shift to his left, toward Phil "Ask him, he knows mo—"

Blood spurts from his throat after I drag the blade across it from ear to ear. I casually shove the full baggie in my pocket and wipe my blade clean on my jeans.

"What the fuck?!" Phil demands, fury in his tone. "Why'd you do that?"

I slowly turn to him and grin. "What did you think was gonna happen Phil? That you were gonna get here and we'd have a tea party?"

"He was just a kid."

"Then maybe he should have thought twice before diving into the deep end where he couldn't swim." I cock my head to the side. "Since when do you give a shit about anyone but yourself, Phil?"

He doesn't answer me, so I crouch down in front of him and hold my knife to his junk. "Now isn't the time to shut your mouth, Phil."

"I'd listen to him if I were you," Magic adds. "I'm pretty sure he hasn't eaten today, which means he's probably a little twitchy. I'm not in the mood to see a botched snip-snip, if you know what I mean."

Phil keeps his face impassive, but he wisely starts talking. "I don't know who's supplying the shit."

"I'm not really buying that. Are you, Magic?"

"Nope."

"You're gonna have to do better than that, Phil," I say, pressing my knife into his groin.

This would be so much more satisfying if Phil would acknowledge the pain I'm causing, but no. He's gotta be all stoic and shit. He'd actually make a decent prospect, ya know, if the circumstances were different.

"All I know is the name Dracula," he says calmly.

"And that's information we already have. What else?"

"He never shows himself. All dealings are through text messages or phone calls where the voice is altered."

I pull my knife back, letting him feel a few moments of hope. It's so much more fun to kill when they have hope in their eyes.

"How do you get the pills?"

"We get a text message with coordinates. He drops the product, and we pick it up."

"That's actually helpful, Phil."

I stand up and sheath my knife. The hope in Phil's eyes practically glows.

"When will you have another pick up?" Magic asks, moving to stand beside me.

Phil shrugs. "I never know exactly when. He gives me enough each time to last a month. As soon as I sell out, he seems to know, and I get a text."

"Does he text the phone I took from you earlier?" Magic asks.

Phil nods.

"I think we're done here," I say to Magic and we both start toward the door.

"Thank you, Phil," Magic says. "We owe you one."

Phil, the cocky fucker, laughs. "Don't think I won't collect. I'm sure I'll think of something you can do for me."

I pause and pull the baggie of pills out of my jeans pocket. "Gimme a sec, Magic. I forgot something."

As I march back to Phil, I snag a handful of the red coated death candies out of the plastic. I reach out to force his jaw open before shoving the pills down his throat and covering his mouth and nose so he has no choice but to swallow. Once he does, I pat his cheek.

"There, that should hold you over."

"What the hell? That shit'll kill me." I ignore him all the way to the door. There's a pause and then a worried, "Hey, where are you going? You're not gonna leave me here, are you?"

I pull on the door to close it and chuckle. "We'll be right back. Promise."

Phil's frantic shouts disappear the moment the door clicks into place.

"Please tell me we're not going back in there," Magic groans.

"Fuck no, we're not. We're gonna leave him there to enjoy the high until it kills him."

"And I thought I was cruel."

"You are," I tell him. "But so am I."

Magic hands me my cut and I put it on.

"Thanks for letting me take the lead again, bro."

"No problem. But don't forget I'm the enforcer. Once you work out whatever you need to work out, the kills become mine again."

"Agreed. I'll even let you burn this one. Come back in two hours and make sure the pills did the trick, then burn him."

"And if the pills didn't work?"

"Burn him."

"Can I play a little first?"

"I don't give a rat's ass. As long as he's in the pit before you're done, I'm good."

It doesn't take us long to walk through the woods toward our cabins. When we reach the edge of the property, my phone rings. I don't recognize the number but answer it anyway.

"Yo," I say by way of greeting.

"I'd like to thank you for taking care of our mutual problem." The voice is robotic, altered.

I grab Magic's arm to stop him from walking any further, and then I put the call on speaker.

"But for future reference, every kill you make moving forward will result in the death of someone you love."

My vision blurs to a hazy red. "Dracula," I push out. I don't ask because I know it's him. It has to be him.

"Yes, I am Dracula. And you are Mason 'Duck' Howard, VP of Satan's Legacy MC. Oh, and a new father too."

"What the fuck?" Magic mouths. He's got his own cell out and he's texting, no doubt filling in Snow.

"You leave my daughter out of this you sick fuck," I seethe.

"I make no promises."

"What do you want?" I ask, hoping to get something, anything, from him.

"What I want is none of your concern. Quit trying to figure out who I am. Stop killing my people. Let my red beauties run freely through Denver."

"Not gonna happen," I snarl.

"Then people will die. People you care about. And their blood will be on your hands." He laughs and the robotic sound sends a chill down my spine. "I wonder, who should I focus on first? It definitely won't be your daughter. I mean, c'mon, even I'm not that big of a monster. But what about your best friend or better yet, that cunt of a nurse you moved into your cabin?"

"If you come after anyone, you seal your fate. I will end you."

"No, you won't," he says. "You have the power to stop this, Duck. Consider yourself warned."

The line goes dead, and I'm left standing there, vibrating with rage. I look toward my place, itching to run and check on Grace and Daisy. Logic tells me they're fine, but until I see them with my own eyes...

"Go," Magic says. "I'll fill Snow in and have him call church."

"Thanks, man."

I sprint to my cabin and crash through the door at a dead run, stopping only when I turn down the hall and see Grace coming out of Daisy's room and pulling the door shut. She twists my way and jumps.

"Shit, you scared me," she accuses with a hand to her chest.

My heart is racing, and I swear I can feel the blood whooshing through my veins.

"Is Daisy okay?" I rasp.

"Yeah." Grace's eyes fill with concern when she takes in my bloody clothes. This is the second time I've come home like this, and it'll be the second time I'll tell her it's club business. "Are you?"

Rather than answer, I close the distance between us in one long stride. Her eyes widen a fraction, but the green sparkles when I cup her cheeks in my dirty hands.

"I'm sorry," I say and run the tip of my nose along the side of hers.

"F-for what?" Her words are breathy, like she can't get enough oxygen.

"For this."

Smashing my mouth against hers, I dart my tongue out to trace the seam of her lips. Grace parts for me and clashes her tongue with mine. Her hands paw at my chest and she fists my shirt, practically ripping it from my body.

She tastes like strawberries and cream mixed with the same amount of desperation that I feel. A taste so addictive that I know I'm now ruined for any other woman for the rest of my life.

I slant my head to deepen the kiss and swallow Grace's needy moans. I absorb her hips as she thrusts them against me, seeking friction where she needs it most.

I want to give her what she wants. My cock begs me to release him. But I can't. Not like this. Grace deserves more than to be devoured by a man covered in the blood of his two latest victims.

With newfound restraint, a restraint that will snap like a guitar string if I don't stop, I pull away. Leaning my forehead against hers, I keep our eyes locked.

"Are you still sorry?" she asks.

I could lie to her and say that I am. I could let her walk away from this encounter with the knowledge that I feel guilty. But I'm selfish, so I do neither of those things.

"No."

"Good." Grace's lips tilt up into a smile. "Because I'm not."

CHAPTER 19
GRACE

An entire week has passed since Duck kissed me. Seven whole days since he told me he wasn't sorry, yet he hasn't made another move. Not that he's had any time. We've barely crossed paths, only communicating through texts. He's rarely here and when he is, his focus is on Daisy.

"As it should be," I coo at her in the swing Laney brought over, saying she had an extra one that Zoe doesn't need.

Daisy gurgles back up at me. Every day that passes, I fall more and more in love with her, which scares the shit out of me. I keep telling myself that she's not mine to love, that Duck will learn how to do this on his own and I won't be needed anymore. But my foolish heart doesn't listen.

"Whaddya say we text Daddy and see if he's going to be home for dinner?"

I lift my phone off the kitchen counter where I left it and open up my messaging app.

Me: Daisy wants to know if you'll be home for dinner tonight.

Duck: Doubt it. Something came up. I'll check on her when I do roll in.

I sigh and look at Daisy. "Sorry baby girl. Daddy's gonna be late again."

Daisy scrunches up her face like she understands me and isn't the least bit happy with that bit of information. I snap a picture and send it to Duck.

Duck: That's low, trying to guilt trip me like that.

Me: If you're feeling guilty, that's on you.

Duck: Grace, please...

Me: Please what?

Duck: Never mind. I'll get home as soon as I can, but it likely won't be before you're both in bed.

Now it just feels like he's avoiding me. It would make sense. Maybe he really does regret that kiss but doesn't know how to tell me. Taking the bull by the horns, I type out another text.

Me: Are you avoiding me?

Those three dots taunt me as he types out a response. It takes him so long that I'm beginning to think he's writing a damn book. Then the dots disappear and my phone rings.

Before I can get a word out, Duck blurts, "What makes you think I'm avoiding you?"

"Oh, I don't know, the fact that the only communication we've had all week is through texts. I thought..." Sighing, I let my words trail off.

"You think I'm regretting kissing you. Is that it?"

"Well, yeah. What else am I supposed to think?"

"Grace, I meant it when I said I wasn't sorry. I don't regret kissing you at all. Things are just insane right now with the club and it's keeping me away."

Doubt lingers. "Are you sure that's it?"

"Trust me. If I could be there with you right now, I would be. Not gonna lie and say that doesn't scare me, but my fear doesn't make it any less true."

"Why does it scare you?"

"Are you kidding? It's not like I've had the best track record with women recently."

"I'm not Heather," I remind him.

"No, you're not. But you're also being paid to be there. How am I supposed to know if you're there because you want to be or if it's because of the money?"

Anger rises to the surface, clouding my thoughts. He has a point, but couldn't he have said something? Probably not, because he's a man and men are stubborn.

"I guess we both have some issues."

When Duck sighs, I imagine he's also running a hand through his hair. "Listen, I really wish I had more time to talk right now, but we're about to ride out. I promise I'll carve out time in the morning to finish this conversation, okay?"

"Yeah, okay."

"And Grace?"

"Hmm?"

"You don't have to wait for me to make a move. You can make one too."

Duck disconnects the call and I'm left standing there, staring at the screen. Before I can think about what he said, there's a knock on the door.

"Dang, Daisy, we're popular today," I joke as I pass her on my way to see who it is.

After opening it, I beam a smile at Little Man, a club prospect. I've seen him around the clubhouse when Daisy and I make our way over there to meet with Sami, Fallon, and Laney. I like Little Man. He's clearly loyal to the club and takes his position as a prospect very seriously.

"What can I do for ya, LM?"

He rolls his eyes at my nickname for him. I know he doesn't particularly like it, but he tolerates it, just like he tolerates all the teasing the other women give him.

Little Man hands me an envelope. "This came in the mail for you."

"Man of few words today, huh? Must be a requirement to join Satan's Legacy."

"Huh?"

I chuckle to myself. "Nothing."

"Right. So, need anything while I'm here?"

"Nope. Daisy and I are good to go. Gonna rustle up some dinner and then give her highness a bath and a bottle, and then it'll be bedtime."

Little Man just stares at me like I've lost my mind. I decide to take pity on him.

"No, LM, we're good. But thank you for asking."

"You're welcome. I'll be at the clubhouse if you need anything. I know Duck and the others are out tonight, but you're never alone here."

"I know. And thank you. I appreciate that."

Little Man nods and then walks away.

I shut and lock the door before dropping the letter on the coffee table. I'll deal with it later, once Daisy's asleep. Until then, she's my priority.

It takes thirty minutes or so to make some spaghetti and garlic bread. I sit on the floor next to Daisy's swing and talk nonsense to her while I eat. When I'm done, I feed her.

After Daisy's bath, I snuggle with her in the recliner until I'm confident she won't wake up and then I put her in her crib so I can finish cleaning up the mess in the kitchen. I dish up a plate for Duck and put it in the microwave, like I do every night.

It's not lost on me that since I've moved in, we function like a family. Him off at work and me acting as the stay-at-home mom who has very little life outside of hearth and home. And then there's Daisy, the perfect daughter who completes the perfect picture.

Only it's not perfect. Duck thinks the only reason I'm here is because I'm paid to be here. and I'm still not sure if and when he's gonna toss me to the curb like Carter did. Yeah, definitely not perfect.

But maybe, just maybe, I can fix one of those problems. I dash to my bedroom and yank open the top drawer of my dresser. Reaching underneath my bras and panties, I pull out the locked bank bag Snow gave me on my first day here.

Back in the kitchen, I set the bag on the counter, where I know Duck will see it, and write the code to open it on a slip of paper for him. I don't bother opening the bag because I know exactly how much money is in there. One hundred thousand dollars and not a penny less. Snow promised to pay me double and he did, giving me six months' worth upfront. He said we'd discuss the next payment after I'd been here five months. I haven't touched it and never planned to.

Hopefully, that will rid Duck of some of his fear. If not, then I'm not really sure what else I can do to prove to him that I'm here because I want to be.

I breathe a little easier knowing I've taken a step forward when it comes to Duck. I know it doesn't make sense, but I'm falling for him just as much as his daughter, and I hate that he doesn't know it.

Right, because you've told him so many times.

"Oh, shut it," I mumble to myself.

Satisfied that it's all I can do for now, I start a load of laundry and then curl up on the couch to watch something on Netflix. I hit play on a movie I've seen dozens of times, but then the discarded letter catches my eye.

I stare at the envelope, trying to discern whose handwriting it is, but I have no clue. And there's no return address, so that doesn't help either. I pull out a single piece of lined paper, filled with barely legible writing.

Grace (or cunt as I like to refer to you),

I hope this letter finds you well. Wait, no, that's a lie. I hope you're as miserable as I am. Only, I guess I'm not miserable, not now that I'm no longer living a life I never wanted. I know you think that you're well rid of me, but surprise, you're not. I thought I made it clear that I'd ruin you if you fucked with me, but apparently you don't listen.

That will be your downfall. I have far more resources than Satan's Legacy could ever dream of having, so I suggest you find a better place to hide. Because I'm coming for you. When you least expect it, when you're completely happy for the first time in your stupid life, I'll be there to burn it all to the ground. I'll enjoy every second leading up to the moment the life drains from your body. I'm pretty sure your new fuck buddy won't enjoy the show as much as me, but that doesn't matter. It'll be enough that he won't have the will to live, let alone the strength to come after me. Not after I take everything from him.

Your #1 Enemy

I barely make it to my bathroom before retching until there's not an ounce of anything left in my stomach.

CHAPTER 20

DUCK

I managed to get home earlier than I thought, but it's still past midnight and dark as fuck out. Flickering light shines through the windows, letting me know that Grace is either watching Netflix or she fell asleep watching it. The image of her curled up on the couch puts a smile on my face.

But it doesn't last. I still have to go inside and face her after our brief phone call. I stopped by the clubhouse to check in with Little Man, as he was put in charge of keeping an eye on things while most of the patched members were out. He said everything was fine and that he even spoke to Grace when he brought her a piece of mail she received.

Most of the guys stayed at the clubhouse, craving the relief liquor would bring them. It was a rough run. We'd gotten a tip from one of our runners, who'd heard what happened to Kenny and Phil and wanted no part of that. He told us that Dracula was supposed to make a drop to restock his pills, but we waited for hours at the location our guy provided and the fucker never showed.

Whether our guy lied, or Dracula found out, we'll never

know. Magic wanted to take our guy out, but after a quick field vote, it was decided to let him be... for now. With Dracula's threat against the people I care about, we're being careful. I understand it, but I don't like it.

Shoving all thoughts of the club aside, I dismount my Harley and head for the door. As soon as I step inside, I know something is horribly wrong.

Daisy is crying, but it sounds hoarse, making me question how long it's been since she started. I race to the nursery and grab her out of her crib before heading to Grace's room, whispering assurances to my little girl the entire time. Grace would never let Daisy cry that long, unless she didn't have a choice.

Dracula's threat rings in my ears as I knock on Grace's door. "Grace," I call out. I hear muffled sounds coming from her room, but I can't make out what they are. My knocking turns into pounding and I yell louder. "Grace, are you okay in there?"

Still, she doesn't answer. I check the knob and find it locked, so I do the only thing I can do: kick the fucker down. Daisy cries louder, although I'm not even sure how that's possible at this point. As soon as the broken door collapses onto the carpet, the muffled sounds I was hearing become unmistakable.

I rush to the en suite and confirm what I already knew. Grace is in the shower, but she's curled up in the fetal position and huddled in the corner. She's sobbing incoherently, her voice hoarser than Daisy's. Her skin is red, and I spot a few blisters forming.

I know I need to get Grace outta there, but I can't take care of Daisy and her at the same time. I reach into my cut and grab my cell so I can shoot off a quick text to Snow.

Need u now. Bring Sami.

I toss the device on the floor in the bathroom, not giving a shit if it breaks or not. I kneel by the shower and try to talk to Grace.

"Grace, I'm here," I tell her. "It's Duck. Can you hear me?"

She gives no indication that she's hearing anything.

"C'mon, Grace. I need you to come out of there. I'd drag you out, but I've got Daisy in my arms."

A minute later, my front door slams open and within seconds, Snow is barreling into Grace's bathroom with Sami on his heels.

"Aw, fuck," Snow mutters. "I was wondering when this would happen."

I whip my head up at him. "What the hell does that mean?"

"You're about to find out."

Sami pushes past Snow and reaches for Daisy. "Here, give her to me. I'll take her to our house and get her calmed down. You focus on Grace."

I smile weakly at her. "Thanks." Sami leaves the bathroom and Snow begins to follow her, but I snag his wrist. "Would you mind staying?"

"Not at all. I'll be in the living room."

I nod my thanks and return all my attention back to Grace. She was already scaring the shit out of me, but the fact that she hasn't reacted in the slightest to Snow and Sami being here adds fuel to my fear.

Reaching into the shower, I check the water temperature and hiss when I find it freezing. Jesus, how long has she been in here? Turning the water off, I notice that, not only is she sobbing and burned, but she's also shivering.

I try to move my arms under her body so I can lift her out, but that's when her brain comes back online, and she flails her arms and legs. I take a kick to the chin and fall back on my ass.

"I-I'm sorry," she mumbles through her sobs. "I k-k-killed her."

"Grace, baby, it's me. It's Duck."

"S-sorry. He's b-b-back."

I plead with her to hear me and to stop thrashing before she hurts herself, but she doesn't. She's trapped inside her head, fighting like hell to make it through whatever nightmare or memory she's stuck in. I try several more times, but each time results in another injury to either her or me that will need to be addressed.

"Snow!" I bellow, needing him in here fast.

Grace doesn't flinch, just continues to thrash and repeat the same thing over and over: Sorry, I killed her, and he's back. Snow is by my side in seconds, keeping his gaze averted from her naked body. I appreciate the thought, but he's gonna have to look at her to help me. He gets a free pass on this one.

"I need you to help me get her outta here."

"I think we're both going to have to get in there."

"Ya think?" I snap. "Let's just do it already."

We step inside the shower, and crouch down. Snow is at her back, and I'm in front. After dodging several blows, Snow gets his arms wrapped around her in an effort to keep her still. Grace isn't able to swing her arms around, but she doesn't have the same problem with her legs.

"Just grab her ankles," Snow barks. "It might not be the best way, but it'll enable us to carry her out."

I do as he says and the moment we lift her off the shower floor, her body goes limp. As much as I hated the fight she was putting up, I think this is worse. Because now it's like she's got no fight left.

We get her to the bed and set her down.

"I'm gonna call Carnie and have him come check her out."

Snow disappears into the hallway, leaving me to keep trying to calm Grace down.

Everything in me wants to strip down and share my body heat with her, but I'm hesitant because of her burns. I don't know how bad they are, and I don't want to risk making them worse.

"S-s-sorry," Grace cries. "C-cold."

"Fuck it," I mutter.

Quickly stripping out of my clothes, I toss them to the floor before crawling in beside Grace and wrapping her in my arms.

"I'm here, Grace." I kiss her head. "I'm right here."

She continues to cry, but now she's no longer doing it alone. I don't know how much time passes before Carnie strolls into the room, but it can't be too long because he's a quick motherfucker.

"No one told me I was gonna need to scrub my eyes clean after this visit," he jokes.

"Keep it up and you'll have to scrub a lot more than that."

"Okay, okay, not in the mood for jokes."

"Jesus, Carn, did you really think I would be?"

"What seems to be the problem?" he asks, slipping into doctor mode.

"She's got burns from the shower and probably some other injuries. She fought Snow and me when we tried to get her out. She's also shivering like a mad woman and crying so hard I worry there's no fluid left in her body."

He digs around in his medical bag before pulling out a vial and syringe. "I'm gonna need you to stay there while I administer this sedative. Once that kicks in, you'll need to skedaddle so I can give her a thorough exam."

"I'm not leaving her, Carnie," I snap.

"Yeah, D, you are." I look over my shoulder and see Snow standing in the doorway. "Let him do his job. As soon as he's done, you can come back in and be with her."

Words of protest sit on the tip of my tongue, but I hold them back. Snow's right. I wanna throat punch him for it, but that won't make it any less true.

"Fine."

Carnie walks to the other side of the bed and kneels on the mattress. "Okay, Grace. You're gonna feel a little pinch."

She doesn't hear a word he says, but that won't stop Carnie from talking. After he injects the sedative, he rubs the area with his thumb to soothe the site.

"There ya go, Grace. You'll start feeling better in no time."

Carnie tosses the used syringe in his bag so he can take it back to the clubhouse and dispose of it properly. Then he sits in the chair in the corner while we wait for the drugs to do their job.

It only takes about ten minutes for Grace to stop crying and drift to sleep. Snow grips my shoulder and pulls me off the bed.

"C'mon. Get dressed and come into the living room so Carnie has room to work."

I go through the motions on autopilot, only to jolt to awareness when I find Snow pacing the living room with a murderous look on his face and a piece of paper scrunched in his fist. Good, because I'm feeling pretty fucking stabby myself.

"Wanna tell me what the fuck that was about?" I shout at him.

I'll give the man credit. Guilt flashes in his eyes for a split second before he masks it. "How should I know?"

I grab Snow by his cut and slam him against the wall. He's not my president right now. He's my best friend who I thought would tell me everything, especially when it comes to my woman.

Your woman?

"Sure sounded like you knew when you said you were wondering when it was going to happen," I snarl.

"Remember who you're talking to, D."

"I know exactly who I'm talking to... a pussy ass bitch who is keeping secrets from me."

Pain ricochets around in my skull from the blow to my head that Snow delivers. I stumble to the side, losing my grip on him, giving him a chance to reverse our positions.

"It's not my story to tell." His tone is deceptively calm. But I'd recognize the very short leash on his anger anywhere. "Besides, I'm not sure this has anything to do with what she told me." He lets go of my cut and slaps the piece of paper to my chest. "This was on the floor."

I read the letter, the one Little Man must have brought her, and the further into the words I get, the more confused I become.

"Who would write this?" I ask, more to myself than Snow. "Grace couldn't possibly have any enemies."

"I'm not convinced she does."

"You're gonna have to explain that because my brain is too maxed out to follow."

Snow leans against the couch and crosses his arms over his chest. "Think about it. You get a phone call a week ago, presumably from Dracula, and then we magically get a lead

145

on the fuckstick, only to have it not pan out. Then you come home to this. He's playing us, D. He's gotta be."

"I need more, man, because it still doesn't make sense."

Snow sighs in exasperation. "Duck, my gut tells me that Dracula set up everything. After he called you, he wanted to see if he could draw you out. So, he made sure we were given info about a drop. We fell for it. I'm guessing he sent this letter so he knew it would get here at the perfect time. And he did it because he assumed we'd kill our runner for lying to us. He told you he was coming after people you care about if anyone else died. Maybe he wanted to give Grace a similar warning."

"That makes no sense, Prez. We didn't kill anyone. We let the runner go. There's gotta be another explanation." I snap my fingers. "Wait, Grace kept saying 'he's back'. Who the fuck is he?"

"I don't know, but Duck, she was delirious. Certainly not thinking clearly."

"Yeah, maybe."

"Look, do you have any other explanation?"

"No." My shoulders sag. "None of this makes a lick of sense."

"Crazy rarely does, brother." Snow pushes off the couch and wanders into the kitchen. I follow. He digs in the fridge until he finds the beer and pulls two out, handing me one of them.

I take a swig and when I set the bottle on the counter, a bank bag with a note catches my eye.

"What's this?" I ask as I lift it.

Snow glances at it and rolls his eyes. "Knowing you like I do, I'm guessing that's the money I paid Grace when she moved in. Please tell me you didn't say something stupid to her about the arrangement."

I think back over my phone conversation with Grace and groan when I remember what I said about her being here. Fuck, that feels like a lifetime ago.

"You did, didn't you?" Snow prompts.

Shoving a hand through my hair, I mumble, "Maybe."

Snow tips back his beer and drains whatever's left. "This is the day that just keeps on giving."

Carnie strolls into the kitchen just then, looking as tired as I feel. "She's all set," he says, scrubbing a hand over his face. "The burns aren't as bad as they looked. I put some salve on the few blisters and left a tube of it on the night-stand. Use it for a few days and those should heal nicely."

"Any other injuries?" I ask.

"Some bumps and bruises, but those will heal on their own." Carnie looks between Snow and me. "Emotionally, that's a whole other ball game. There are some things my medicine can't heal."

I nod, distracted by the need to go to Grace. Carnie must sense it.

"Go be with her, D," he says. "She'll sleep for a few more hours at least. But she's gonna need someone when she wakes up. Whatever caused this, it's deep in her soul. She's not gonna be able to find her way out of it on her own."

I think about the letter, about how scared she must have been when she read it. My brain can't accept that it was that letter alone that sent Grace spiraling. But until she wakes up, all I have is Snow's theory and my worries.

"She won't be alone," I vow.

"Good. Now, I'm beat. If you need me, you know how to find me."

After Carnie leaves the cabin, Snow starts toward the door, but stops and turns back around to face me.

"Duck, I'm only gonna say this once and then it's up to

you to take things from here." His face is somber but determined. "Grace has been through enough in her life." I open my mouth to question him, but he holds a hand up. "Not my story," he reminds me. "If you think there's even the slightest chance that you're gonna send her packing someday, tell me now. I'll help her find another place to live and we'll figure everything out for Daisy. Otherwise, man up and be the person Grace needs you to be."

The thought of Grace not being here hits me like a cattle prod. I don't like it at all. I don't know if we're heading toward forever, but I know I want to find out. If things don't work out, I'll deal with Snow's wrath then.

"She stays."

CHAPTER 21
GRACE

W hy am I trapped? There's a heavy bar lying across my stomach and my legs are bound together by...

Another leg?

I force my eyes open and groan as the sunlight streaming in the window stabs into my vision. I'm able to move my head from side to side, so I quickly determine that I'm in my bedroom and my own bed. And I'm being held in place, not by a bar, but by Duck's arm and leg, both of which are casually draped over me.

"You awake?"

I narrow my eyes at him. "Why are you in here?" Another detail registers. "And why am I naked? What's going on?"

My voice is raspy, like my throat is swollen and raw. But why?

"You don't remember?" he asks as he sits up and leans against the headboard.

His chest is bare and when I lower my eyes, the head of his cock is peeking out from beneath the sheet... and I'm eye level with it. I try to sit up, by my entire body aches and feels as if it's on fire.

"Here, let me help you." Duck gently slides me up and maneuvers me to sit between his legs before guiding me back to lean against him. "Better?"

"Mmm, yes. Why do I feel like I've been hit by a bus and swallowed razors?"

"You really don't remember?"

I shake my head. "No, I... The last thing I remember is Little Man stopping by with a letter."

Apparently the word 'letter' is all it takes to trigger my memories because one by one, they slam into my brain and lock into place. I try to scramble away from Duck, frantic to get away, but he only tightens his hold.

"I have to get out of here," I cry. "You don't understand. He's back. I don't want you or Daisy to get hurt. I've gotta go."

"Grace, stop," Duck says firmly. "You're not going anywhere. You're safe here."

"No, I'm not. Not if he's found me." I press my palm to my forehead. "I don't understand. It's been five years. Not a word in five years and now he wants to be a dick."

"Grace, calm down. I can't help you if you don't tell me what's going on."

"The letter. He sent me a letter. I have no idea how he knew where to mail it, but still, he sent it." Another thought occurs to me. "Oh my God, where's Daisy? Why isn't she crying? What did he—"

Duck covers my mouth with his hand. "Shhh. Daisy is fine. She's with Snow and Sami. They came and got her after I found you in the shower last night."

"Oh."

"Listen, I think the first thing we need to do is get some

coffee. Then we're going to sit here and talk about what happened last night, who this *he* is, why Snow knows your secret and I don't, and the letter. Sound good?"

"Can't we just stand on hot coals for a few hours? That sounds like more fun."

Duck chuckles as he places a kiss on my head. "No, we can't." He scoots out from behind me and stands. "I'll be back in a few minutes. Don't move."

He doesn't give me a chance to protest. Not that I'd be able to with him walking away butt ass naked. Damn that man has a nice ass.

I know he told me not to move, but I have to pee. I scramble off the bed and quickly realize that scrambling isn't the best idea. Every inch of me is sore. Going a little more slowly, I take care of business, wash my hands and brush my teeth, and then crawl back into bed.

As I'm pulling the sheet over my body, Duck strolls back in with two mugs of coffee and a t-shirt draped over his shoulder. He's still naked. He sets the mugs on the night-stand, and I think he's about to put the shirt on himself, but he surprises me.

"Here, let me help you sit up." And I do let him, although I now know I can do it on my own. "Arms up." When I comply, he slips the shirt over my head. "There, now I can focus on talking without the distraction of your tits."

It's a good thing I haven't taken a sip of coffee because I would have spit it out at that comment.

"What are you gonna do about..." I tip my head at his crotch. "... that distraction?"

"Do you want me to do something about it?" he taunts.

I highly doubt this is the direction he wants our conversation to go in, but if I can keep stalling, I will.

"Not really."

Duck cocks his head. "Are you trying to distract me?"

"Maybe."

"Hold that thought." Duck races from the room and returns a moment later with sweats on. "Better?"

"No."

"Too bad. We really do need to talk."

I reach for my mug and take a sip, savoring the way the hot liquid warms my insides. "Then talk."

Duck sits next to me on the mattress. "I don't even know where to start. I guess..." He takes a deep breath, then another and another. "I guess I'll start with that bag of money I found in the kitchen. Why'd you put it there?"

Oh, right. I did do that.

"I wanted to prove to you I wasn't here just because of the money. I figured if you saw that it's all still there, you might believe me."

"Okay. First of all, I'm sorry I said that. I have some hang ups since Heather that make me question things. But those are my issues, not yours."

"No, Duck, you're wrong. If they're your issues, they're my issues." I slowly shift so I'm facing him. "Sure, when Snow originally asked me to move in here, I accepted that he was going to compensate me for it. I thought it was a job."

"Do you still feel like it's a job?"

"No. I haven't since the moment Snow told you you had them add that bathroom and closet. I realized that you did that for me. You might have been acting like an ass, but you still thought about me enough to make sure I was comfortable here, that I was at home here. That means a lot."

"He shouldn't have told you that."

"But he did. And even if he hadn't, I'd still be in the same boat as I am now."

"What boat is that?"

"The 'I like you' boat. I didn't want to. Not even the tiniest bit. Yet here we are. I can't explain it, but I'm drawn to you. And I love Daisy like she was my own."

Realizing what I just said, I clamp my mouth shut and slap a hand over it. Tears well in my eyes and spill onto my cheeks.

Duck uses his thumbs to wipe the tears away, but they're coming too fast for him to keep up. "Aw, Grace, what is it? Why are you crying?"

I don't answer him right away. I can't, not with emotion clogging my throat. Rather than push me, he sits there quietly, watching me, waiting. When I'm all cried out, a strange sense of acceptance washes over me. I take a deep breath and tell him my story.

"I'm a mother," I say quietly. "Did you know that?"

"No. Had we known, the offer to come live here would have extended to your child."

I shake my head sadly. "It's a nice thought, but my daughter is dead."

Duck rears back at that. "What? How?"

"Stillborn."

"Jesus, I can't even imagine."

"No one can, unless they've lived it." I ground my palms against my eyes. "Anyway, as soon as she was born, my fiancé, Carter, went nuts. Blamed me saying I was worthless and couldn't do anything right. The things he said..." I shudder. "I can't even begin to explain how cruel he was. When I was discharged from the hospital, Carter came and picked me up. All I wanted to do was go home and cry, but instead, he took me to a rundown apartment building. He'd rented an apartment, paid the security deposit and first month's rent. He told me that it was my new home and then beat me to make sure I understood."

"I'll fucking kill him," Duck snarls.

I rest my hand on his arm, offering him comfort while also taking my own. "Long story short, Carter broke off our engagement. I was permitted to go to the funeral, but he made it very clear that he didn't want to see me again after that. I found out later, through some friends, that he was only with me because of what he thought I could give him. When our daughter was stillborn, I guess he figured I wasn't worth the hassle of pretending he loved me anymore." I shrug as if it no longer matters. "I'm over Carter. I was the second he walked out of that apartment, leaving me to suffer alone. But I'm not over everything else. I missed out on so much, Duck. I used to visit my little girl's grave in the middle of the night so I wouldn't run into anyone. I did that every night for a few months and then I realized I needed to stop. I applied for a traveling nurse position and was sent here, where I chose to stay."

Rather than say anything, Duck gently pulls me into his arms and holds me. His muscles are tense, but he keeps himself in check.

"I don't know why Carter is contacting me now, or even how he found me, but I'm too afraid to find out. There was a time I thought he hung the moon, but now all I know is he's a man who doesn't care who he hurts as he climbs his way to the top."

"He'll never lay a finger on you again. I promise you that," Duck says with conviction. "He'd have to go through me first."

"I appreciate that, but it won't come to that. Duck, he

threatened you. I can't let him get to you or Daisy. I've already lost one daughter. I can't lose another."

Duck leans back to look into my eyes. "You see Daisy as your daughter?"

"Yeah, I do. I know I didn't give birth to her, but I've been there from day one. I fell in love with her immediately, despite telling myself over and over again why I shouldn't. That's why I initially told Snow no when he asked me to move in here. I knew it would only end in more heartbreak."

"Let me guess... he pushed and pushed until you told him your story."

"Don't be mad at him. He meant well."

"I'm not mad. Honestly, I'm grateful."

"You are?"

"Of course, I am," Duck insists. "I know I should be running for the hills after what Heather did. But with you, I can't seem to fight hard enough to keep you at a distance. Now, I don't want to fight it."

"So now what?" I ask, unsure of what to make of this.

Duck shrugs. "I don't know. I think we take it one day at a time."

"I can do that."

Duck grins. "Good. Now, I'm assuming you think Carter sent the letter."

"Who else would it be?" I burrow deeper into Duck's chest. "As soon as I finished reading it, I puked my guts up. Everything that happened five years ago came flooding back and I needed to get it out of my system. Then I ended up in the shower because I wanted to erase any trace of him that remained. I know it's illogical, but..."

"But you felt dirty somehow," he finishes for me. "I'm so sorry that you went through that experience and that it got dredged up again. Sorrier than I can ever convey. But I don't think that letter was from Carter. Snow and I have a theory."

"Club business, right?" I snap, frustration slipping in.

"Yes, but I'm going to fill you in on some of it since you're now smack dab in the middle of it."

"I'm listening."

"Satan's Legacy has enemies, but most recently, there's a new drug being pushed on the streets that's killing people and taking away our business."

"Wait. Are you talking about those red pills with the bats on them?"

Duck arches a brow. "How'd you know?"

"The ER deals with a lot of overdoses. And in the last eight months or so, those numbers have increased. We would find baggies of those pills on some of the patients. The cops say they're looking into it, but obviously, they're not getting very far."

"And they won't. This guy, Dracula, is good. If we're struggling to find and identify him, no way the cops will be able to."

"Okay, so what does this have to do with the letter?"

"Well, I got a call from Dracula last week. He made some threats that lead us to believe he sent the letter to prove his point."

"He threatened me?" Duck nods. "But why?"

"Because he wants to hurt me for some reason. I don't know. We're not sure about a lot of things other than he's obviously dangerous and good at what he does."

"Are we safe here? Is Daisy safe?"

"This compound is the safest place you could be."

"If you say so."

"I do."

"So how is the club gonna catch this guy? When will all this be over?"

"I wish I knew, Grace. Believe me when I tell you, we're doing everything we can, and we won't stop until he's no longer an issue."

"In other words, when you find him, you'll kill him."

Those words leave my mouth far easier than they should, and I can't find it in me to care. If this guy is threatening me, threatening Daisy, then he needs to die. Period. Full stop.

"Yes, we'll kill him," Duck confirms.

I nod. "Good."

CHAPTER 22

DUCK

Grace and I sat in silence for a while longer, content in the knowledge that we're on the same page, before I helped her in the shower. It was the longest ten minutes of my life, being so close to her, both of us naked as the day we were born. I couldn't stop my dick from noticing, but I refused to cross that line. Grace deserves better than that.

We spent most of the day talking and binging New Girl on Netflix. I wanted to keep things light. And it seemed to work because Grace was much more relaxed as the day went on.

Every minute with her today felt good. It felt natural. Some would probably say we're nuts, while others might think it odd that we went from forcing our interactions to genuinely caring about one another in the blink of an eye. And who knows? Maybe they're right.

All I know is, I don't fucking care. She has her hooks dug so deep into me and I have no intention of trying to pull them out. What can I say? When that particular lightning bolt strikes, it strikes, and there's not a goddamn thing you can do to stop it. Might as well hold on and ride the current.

"How's she doin'?" Snow asks me when I sit on the stool next to him at the bar in the clubhouse.

"She's okay. She's sleeping again. I really appreciate Sami keeping Daisy another night."

"Don't mention it. We love having her." He sips his beer. "So, judging by the look on your face, she told you everything."

Little Man steps in front of us. "Can I get you anything, D?"

"Double shot of Jack."

"Coming right up."

After Little Man sets my shot in front of me and walks back to the other end of the bar, I return my focus to Snow.

"Yeah, she told me everything. She was convinced it was her ex that sent the letter."

"It wasn't." I quirk a brow at him in question. "What? You didn't seriously think I was gonna let her move onto the compound and not run a background check, did you?"

"Honestly, it never crossed my mind."

"Which just goes to show how fucked up in the head you were." He pauses and takes a sip of his beer. "I'd already run a basic check before I asked her to move in with you and Daisy, but after she told me about her daughter, I dug a little deeper. Wasn't hard to trace her ex, what with articles in the paper about a stillborn baby. Fucking reporters had a field day with that and then covering the funeral. After all, the father was from a prominent family, a family that got off on publicity."

"He beat her, Zeke." I don't use his given name a lot, but sometimes when I just need him to be my friend, it slips out. "She'd just been released from the hospital after delivering a dead baby and he fucking put his hands on her." I lift my shot glass and down the double shot, slamming it on the bar when I'm done. "He banished her to a shit apartment and cut her loose like she was some washed up piece of trash. He used her, and when she failed to give him what he wanted, he punished her."

"Damn. I hadn't known all that. Seems she left a lot of details out when she told me."

"Can you blame her?" I counter.

"No. I wouldn't want to share that with people."

Snow raises his hand to Little Man to signal for him to bring us each another drink. When the beer and shot glass are in front of us, he continues.

"Anyway, I figured it couldn't hurt to see where Carter is now. I didn't really think he was a threat, but there was also Daisy to think about and I couldn't take that chance. Carter definitely isn't a threat. A fuckwad cunt, but not a threat. He's married now and has two sons. Works for his daddy, the local prosecutor. He's got what he wants. Grace doesn't even exist for him anymore."

"Nice," I mumble and then down my second shot.

"Did you tell her about Dracula and the threats?" he asks me.

For a moment, I panic, thinking that I'm gonna be in trouble for telling her, but then I remember that the threat concerns her, and we're permitted to tell ol' ladies about stuff that concerns them.

"I did."

"And another one bites the dust." He chuckles as he lifts his beer to his lips.

"Who bit the dust?"

I spin around on the stool and see Dip standing there with a beer in his hand and a smirk on his face.

"Duck here is gonna make Grace his ol' lady," Snow says.

I say nothing. What is there to say? Some part of me must have known when I told Grace about Dracula because I am intimately familiar with our club's bylaws. Ol' ladies are the only people who are allowed to be given information that would normally fall under club business, and *only* when it pertains to them. That's it. That's the only exception.

Dip climbs up onto the bar and bellows out for everyone to be quiet. When he has their full attention, He grins.

"Listen up ladies and gents," he begins. "Our brother Duck finally got himself an ol' lady!"

Cheers and applause fill the main room of the clubhouse. I want to throttle Dip for doing that, but what would be the point? As VP of the club, I can't exactly correct him.

Do you want to?

No, I don't.

Dip jumps to the floor and slaps me on the back. "Honestly, bro, I'm happy for you. Grace seems great and after Heather, you deserve something great."

"Thanks, Dip."

He walks away, disappearing into the crowd. Things return to normal, and Snow and I get back to our conversation.

"I'm gonna pretend you didn't forget the bylaws," he says, giving me a knowing look. "After seeing Grace last night, how wrecked she was, I can't say I wouldn't have done the same thing. She deserves to know about the threats to her. But Duck? Don't forget again. I won't be so forgiving a second time."

"Right. Thanks."

"Now, I think we need to call church and formulate a plan. We need to nail down this Dracula bastard and end his reign of terror once and for all."

"I couldn't agree more."

"The question is, do we do it tonight, or wait until tomorrow?"

"No time like the present."

CHAPTER 23

GRACE

"Stretch, stretch, stretch."

Duck is sitting on the floor with Daisy on a blanket between his legs. He's holding a small toy above her and she's trying to grab it. She's come leaps and bounds, and I am so glad I've been here for it all.

"She's getting close," I say from my spot on the couch.

"Isn't she?" Duck looks over his shoulder at me and smiles.

Fuck, the things that smile does to me. It doesn't matter what brings it out in him, that smile always results in wet panties. We still haven't had sex, but if our make-out sessions are any indication, when we do, it'll be explosive.

We've fallen into a routine in the last month. Duck does his best to be here for breakfast and dinner every day and always carves out one on one time with Daisy. There are times when he's not here because he and the brothers are chasing down leads and hunting Dracula, but I no longer take issue with it.

I've gotten close to the other ol' ladies and watching them has shown me that, even if I don't always understand what's going on, I need to respect it. Because everything this club does, they do out of love and loyalty. Who am I to argue with that?

"Any thoughts on dinner?" Duck asks.

He now has Daisy in his arms and her eyes are slowly drooping. My ovaries scream.

"You," I blurt out.

Heat infuses my cheeks and Duck grins.

"Oh really?"

I never thought I'd want to have another baby. Losing Lynn was too painful. But the longer Duck and I are together, the more I dream about the life we're building and the things I didn't believe I deserved.

We really are taking things one day at a time, but I know I want that to turn into forever. I love Duck and Daisy. I haven't told him yet, but I'm saving that little tidbit of information until this whole Dracula thing is over. I don't want our future to be clouded by all the negativity.

"Grace?"

"Hmm?"

"I lost you there for a minute," he says. "You okay?"

I smile at him. "Sorry, I got lost in thought."

Duck wiggles his eyebrows. "Dirty thoughts, I hope."

"Wouldn't you like to know?"

"Yes," he says emphatically. "I want to know every salacious detail."

Throwing my head back, I laugh. I do that a lot with Duck. Laugh until it hurts. I slide off the couch to sit next to him and rest my head on his shoulder, careful not to bump Daisy.

"Well, first," I begin. "We both strip out of our clothes." I trail a fingertip down his arm, grinning when I feel goosebumps rise. "Then you spread me out on the bed and dip your finger in my pussy to see how wet I am for you." Duck adjusts himself. "I'd beg you for your tongue, and—"

Duck's phone rings and I swear the growl that escapes him is feral.

"I'm gonna kill whoever this is," he snaps. He lifts his phone off the coffee table and his eyes narrow. "Well, well, well..." He taps the screen to answer it and puts the call on speaker. "What do you want?"

"Hi Duck."

"What do you want, Heather?"

"Is that any way to speak to the mother of your child?" she asks.

"Some mother," I mumble as I stand and then lift Daisy out of Duck's arms.

"Who the fuck was that?" Heather demands.

I carry Daisy to her room, wanting to give Duck some privacy, but he follows me.

"Does it matter?" Duck counters.

"Of course it matters," she shrieks.

"No, it doesn't." Duck follows me back out to the living room. I sit while he paces. "Now, what the fuck do you want?"

"I want to see my baby."

Duck snorts. "You mean the one you tried to kill by orchestrating a car accident?"

"Don't be so dramatic, Duck. She lived. No harm, no foul."

I had no intention of saying a word, I swear it, but her cruelty cannot be ignored. I shoot up from the couch and yank the phone out of Duck's hand.

"Listen here you crazy bitch," I seethe. "Yes, your daughter lived. But not because of anything you did. She lived because she's a fighter. She lived because she has a daddy who loves her. She lived because I was there to pick up the pieces of a life you so carelessly destroyed." The more I talk, the wider Duck's grin becomes. "You want to know who's here with Duck? Me. I'm here. The only mother that little girl knows. So take your callous words and shove them up your ass!"

By the time I'm done, I'm panting with rage. I hand Duck the phone and as he grabs it, he uses his other hand to wrap around the back of my neck and pull me into his chest.

"Are you seriously going to let—"

"Heather," Duck interrupts.

"What?"

"What she said."

Heather sputters nonsense for a minute.

"I can't believe I ever thought I was in love with you," Duck spits out. "How did I not see how fucking evil you are?"

"You're one to talk," Heather snaps. "Satan's Legacy isn't exactly made up of choir boys."

"Don't you dare bring the club into this. They all treated you like family and how did you repay that? By trying to eliminate a future club princess and then ditching me while under the arm of another man."

"I hate you!" she screams.

Duck's chuckle holds no humor. "Well, I guess we have something in common then."

"I want to see my daughter."

"Heather, that's not going to happen."

"I'll sue you for custody," she threatens.

"You can try. But remember who you're going up against."

"Oh, I know exactly who I'm up against. Lucky for me, you don't have a damn clue."

I can feel the tension in Duck, the exasperation at even having to deal with this woman. I wrap my arms around his waist, a silent reminder that I'm here.

"I'll make you a deal," Duck says. "I'll consider letting you see her, if you tell me where you are."

"Ha! Like I'm gonna fall for that. I know I betrayed the club. I'm familiar with the punishment for that particular crime."

"Then we have nothing left to say to each other. Go ahead and sue for custody. Just be prepared to lose."

Duck disconnects the call, silencing Heather's shouted words. We hold onto each other for a few minutes before Duck shifts me back so he can look in my eyes. When he doesn't say anything, I can't help but wonder if he's angry with what I said.

"What?" I ask when he continues to stare.

He opens and closes his mouth several times, clearly struggling with what to say. "I... You..." He shakes his head. "I know I should say something profound or apologize or some shit, but the only thought running through my head right now is how fucking hot you were when you tore into her."

"You're not mad?"

Duck grabs my hand and pushes it against his crotch. "Does that feel like I'm mad?"

I grin. "No."

"Grace, I promise we'll talk about that phone call later, but right now, I need you to do one thing for me."

"What's that?"

"Get your ass to the bedroom. Now."

CHAPTER 24

DUCK

The speed with which Grace takes off for the bedroom only makes my cock strain harder against my jeans. I pop my head into the nursery as I follow behind her and grab the baby monitor just in case.

As I cross the threshold of the bedroom, my lungs seize. Grace is stretched out on the bed, legs and arms spread for me. And her clothes are in a pile on the floor.

"Fuck, I could get used to this," I groan.

I set the monitor on my dresser and quickly divest myself of clothes. Palming my dick, I stalk toward the bed until my legs hit the mattress, making sure to keep my eyes on her face. If I look anywhere else, I'll shoot my load before this even begins.

Grace, on the other hand, has no such problem. Her eyes are roaming every inch of me, pausing only at my cock. Her nostrils flare as she slides a hand over one breast, down her stomach and coming to rest at her clit.

"Ah, ah, ahh," I tsk. "That's for me."

Minx that she is, Grace doesn't remove her hand.

168

"Grace, get that hand away from my pussy," I demand.

When she still doesn't obey, I lean over and grip her wrist, squeezing hard enough to get her to move but not so hard as to hurt her.

"Dammit, Duck, do something," she pleads.

"Patience, baby." I place her arm back above her head. "Do not move."

She whimpers, but she keeps her arm in place. I trail my fingers across her collarbone and down between her tits, letting one hand roam to pinch a nipple. Her whimpers grow in intensity.

Needing to taste her, I wrap my hands under her thighs and yank her to the edge of the bed. I kneel in front of her and drape her legs over my shoulders so I can bury my face in her center.

I inhale her scent, committing it to memory so I can relive this moment any time I want. "So sweet." I drag a finger through her slit, gathering her arousal. "So sweet, so wet. All for me."

"Duck, please. I ne... ahhhh."

Her words turn to moans the second my tongue hits her clit. Grace's hips buck when I breach her tight hole with two fingers and her pussy walls clamp down to keep me locked inside. Not that I would go anywhere. Eating Grace is nirvana.

And I do eat her. Like a starving man attacks a steak. I lick her sensitive nub and tease it with flicks of my tongue. All the while, I continue to finger fuck her. My hand and mouth are in perfect concert to send this woman into blissful oblivion.

Grace thrashes her head from side to side, moaning incoherent words as her pelvis pushes back against me, chasing the orgasm she craves so badly.

"Ah, don't stop," she begs. "I'm so close, don't you dare stop."

As much as I want to swallow her pleasure, I need to feel it even more. Without breaking contact with her clit, I pull my fingers out and rise up so I can shove my cock deep inside her. My balls slap her ass, and she detonates.

"Fuck, yes," I growl.

Grace comes so hard, gripping my cock with her tight little cunt, that I see stars. I fuck her while she soars and slow my thrusts as she falls back to Earth. Her eyes drift closed, but I want none of that.

"Look at me, Grace," I command. Her eyes flutter open. "We're not done. I'm gonna make you come again before I let myself take what I need."

"I don't think I—"

I silence her with a bruising kiss. After I get my fill of her mouth, I pull away and pull out. My cock weeps.

Don't you worry. This will be worth it.

"I don't want you to think, Grace. If I'm doing this right, it should be damn near impossible."

She sucks her swollen bottom lip between her teeth and nods.

"Good girl." I flip her onto her stomach. "Ass up, baby."

Grace doesn't hesitate and when she's in position, I crawl to my knees on the bed behind her. With her booty on display, I run my hands over each creamy globe, letting my thumbs tease her crack. I have no intention of delving into that particular hole just yet, but the way her back arches leads me to believe she might not reject the idea in the future.

I lean over her body, dragging my fingertips over her spine and leaving a trail of kisses until I reach her ear.

"Beautiful Grace," I murmur.

I nip at her lobe then suck on it to soothe the sting. Reaching between us, I drag my cock through her dripping pussy lips and bump the tip against her clit. Grace pushes back against me, desperate for more.

Lining my head up with her core, I whisper, "Is this what you want?"

"Y-yes."

"Who am I to deny you?"

I thrust inside her, hard, and drag slowly back out to the tip. Thrust, drag, thrust, drag. Grace's hands fist in the sheets, holding on as each thrust shoves her forward. Her wet heat is addictive and rapidly becoming my favorite drug.

My spine tingles, and I know I won't last much longer. Keeping one hand on her hip, I move the other to her clit.

"I need you to come, baby," I growl.

Two more forceful thrusts, and Grace falls apart. Her clenching pussy pushes me over the edge. Both of us shout as my cum bathes her insides and hers soaks my cock. When there is not a single drop for her to wring out of me, I collapse to the side, pulling her into my arms.

"Holy. Shit."

Grace wiggles that perfect ass into my groin. "I concur."

"Not that I ever want to make you angry, but damn if you angry doesn't turn me the fuck on."

"I'll keep that in mind," she giggles.

We lay there in silence for a few minutes, both content to keep shutting the world out. Grace relaxes against me, and I think she's fallen asleep. At least until she speaks.

"At the risk of making *you* angry, don't you think you should fill the guys in on your call from Heather?"

And this is why I love Grace. She gets me.

Wait. Love?

Fuck, yes. I love her. She understands that the club will always be there, a large part of who I am, and sometimes that means having to do things at the worst possible times.

"Duck?"

"Huh?"

"Did you hear what I said?"

"Oh, yeah." I kiss her on the cheek. "And you're right. I do need to fill them in."

Grace sits up and scoots toward the headboard. "Go do what you need to do, and Daisy and I will be here when you get back."

"Ya know what? Why don't you and I take a quick shower and then the three of us can all head to the club-house together?"

"But you'll be meeting with the guys."

"Yeah, but I'm sure they'd all love to see Daisy. And hopefully it won't take too long."

"Okay. I'm game."

An hour later, we're walking to the clubhouse with Daisy, a diaper bag, a portable crib, and an extra pacifier in both of our pockets.

CHAPTER 25
GRACE

"Gimme, gimme, gimme."

Toga reaches for Daisy the moment we step through the clubhouse door. It's surprisingly quiet in the clubhouse, especially for this time of evening. Usually the bar is full and the music is blaring.

"What's going on, man?" Duck asks. "Where is everyone?"

"You didn't get Snow's text?"

"Uh, we were a little busy."

Toga glances at me and wisely chooses not to comment on my inflamed cheeks. "Right, well, he called church. Told everyone who didn't need to be here to go home."

"Oh, well, I guess I should take Daisy back home."

"Not so fast, Grace," Toga says. "Snow wants you here too."

"Why?"

Toga shrugs. "Don't know." He looks at Duck. "If you didn't get the text, why are you here?"

"You mean aside from the fact that I'm VP and have every right to be here whenever the fuck I want?"

"Yeah, aside from that."

Duck laughs. "I was actually hoping to talk to everyone about a phone call I got."

A bang from the other side of the room has us all facing that way just as Snow pounds the wall again.

"Meeting room, now," he orders. "You too, Grace. And bring that baby with you."

He turns on his heel and disappears down the hallway. The three of us exchange a look before rushing to do as we're told. We reach the room where the club holds church, and I hesitate.

"What's wrong?" Duck asks me, concern lacing his tone.

Toga walks past us, Daisy still in his arms.

"This is a sacred space, right? Like, I'm not supposed to be in there."

"Neither are babies, yet *that* just happened." Duck tilts his head to indicate all the guys oohing and aahing over Daisy. "Besides, the president ordered it, so you're fine."

"It feels wrong somehow."

Duck wraps an arm around my shoulders and pulls me into his side. "You're not doing anything wrong, Grace. I promise."

He guides me into the room. All the chairs around the table start to fill up as the brothers take their seats, until the only two empty ones are to Snow's right. Daisy is now in Snow's arms and when Duck reaches out to take her from him, Snow shakes his head.

"She'll keep me calm," he says.

"You're not seriously ordering me to let you hold my *infant* daughter because you're so pissed that you need *her* to keep you calm?"

"That's exactly what I'm doing," Snow confirms.

Yeah, that's not happening. I push Duck back into his chair and reach for Daisy. "Snow, hand her over slowly and no one gets hurt."

Snow glares at me, but I don't relent. Finally, he passes Daisy to me.

"Thank you," I quip.

"Don't thank me. It'll be your fault when that little girl is subjected to a fuck load of foul language." He smirks. "See, it's already starting."

"Yeah, yeah, you don't scare me. Besides, she needs to learn all those foul words so she can keep up with the lot of you."

Snow snaps his stare to Duck and points a finger at him. "Don't you dare let her go."

"Wasn't planning on it, Prez."

"Hey," Dip shouts from across the table. "I thought she was already his ol' lady."

Duck groans and I glower at him. "What is he talking about?"

"We'll discuss it later," Duck says. "But hold onto that anger, baby." Then he winks at me.

"As fun as this is to watch," Magic interrupts. "Can we get this show on the road? Zoe hasn't been feeling well, Shiloh wants to help and doesn't understand why Laney and I won't let him, and Laney..." He glares at Snow. "You're amazing, beautiful, stubborn as fuck little sister is going to divorce me if I don't get back home to help her out."

Snow's lips twitch as he fights not to laugh. "You heard the man."

"What the patch binds together," Duck begins and the rest of them chime in. "Let no force tear apart. Satan's Legacy now and forever."

"Aw, that's cute," I comment, which earns me glares from all around the table.

"Grace, you are here by invitation. Keep your comments to yourself."

And just like that, I'm pretty sure I poked the bear.

"I called church because we received a letter in the mail that was addressed to the club as a whole." Snow lifts a piece of paper off the table. "All of you have been filled in about the letter Grace received and this seems to be from the same person. Before I dive into this, is there any other business to discuss? And make it quick because apparently our Enforcer is pussy whipped."

Magic growls, but keeps his mouth shut.

Duck stands. "I was headed over to the clubhouse anyway because I got a call from Heather earlier today."

"What'd the bitch want?" Toga asks.

Instinctively, I hold Daisy closer. Duck rests his hand on my shoulder and rubs his thumb against Daisy's cheek.

"She wants to see her daughter," he tells them.

I snort at that, and Snow's eyes cut to mine. "Sorry."

"Go on," Snow orders.

"Anyway, that's what she said. She wants to see Daisy. Heather practically admitted to the accident. I believe her exact words were 'She lived. No harm, no foul.' Grace proceeded to read her the riot act and told her to shove her words up her ass." Duck grins as he very briefly recounts the call. "Then I told her to sue me for custody if that's what she really wanted."

"Like she'd win," Spark snickers.

"Exactly. But I wanted you all to know because if Heather does try to go the legal route,

I'm gonna need all of you to back me up. Courts favor mothers."

"Seems to me, Daisy has a mother," Snow says. "Doesn't she, Grace?"

"Damn right," I agree.

"Still, I can't be too careful."

"Of course not. We're still trying to track down her location."

"Ya know what? I don't even give a shit anymore. I just want her out of my life, out of Daisy's life. If we ever cross paths with her again, I'll get my revenge, but for now, fuck her. She's not going to destroy the life I'm building."

Duck plops in his chair, and I reach across the armrest to hold his hand. I shouldn't be surprised when he so readily interlocks his fingers with mine, but I am. At least here, I am.

"All in favor of letting sleeping dogs lie where Heather is concerned?"

'Ayes' echo around the room.

"Okay. For now, that nasty problem is moved to the back burner. Moving on to the letter." Snow sits in his chair and reads the words out loud.

Satan's Legacy MC pricks,

I've decided to throw you a bone. You have been diligently trying to get to me for quite some time, and I gotta be honest... I'm getting bored. I really thought you'd continue to kill people in the name of finding me, but you haven't. Sure, you've hunted for me, you've ridden the streets of Denver searching for the creature of the night who beats you at every turn. But you haven't killed again. At least not because of me. Which means there's no gratification in killing your people. I guess I'm more tit for tat than I thought.

When I sent that letter to Grace, I was giddy with

anticipation for the murder spree I was sure you all would embark on. Imagine my surprise when that didn't happen. I know you can do better. I know you enjoy violence and mayhem. It's your love language. So why are you pussying out now?

Shit, I can't even complain that you're trying to rid the streets of my little red pills. In fact, my profits are higher than ever because everyone wants the drug that's better than anything else your fucking club can provide. So, thank you for that. I will admit to a minuscule amount of satisfaction with each overdose I cause, but it's not the same.

I NEED MORE!

So, this is me throwing you a goddamn bone in a last-ditch effort to coax you out of your hidey holes. I'm willing to meet with you. (I know you're all gasping and clutching your pearls right about now because let's face it, Dracula's scary.) Anyway, back to my bone.

I'm willing to meet with you. I'd like to make you a proposition that I think will benefit all of us. But I have one condition (I know, I know, that takes the fun away). I will only meet with your VP and Grace. That's it.

Now I know it would be very tempting to flat out turn me down, so I'll leave you with a reminder of my previous threats and this bit of information: Grace is usually home alone with the baby during the day while Duck deals with club business. You all think they're protected, but I've got connections. I guess I could also alleviate my boredom by playing with Grace's friends, Vince and Lucy, but I'd really rather we keep our business private. And one more thing, the underground space you have at the compound, the one where all the brothers, women, and children flock to when there's danger? Yeah, I know about that.

You have four days from the day this letter was mailed to give me an answer. If you're smart and agree to meet under my conditions, send an email with 'When and Where' in the subject line to ivegotyouover-abarrel@drinkmyblood.net.

Public Enemy #1

Duck pounds his fists into the table. "What the fuck?!"

"There's no way we're doing what he wants," Magic snaps.

"I agree," Toga adds. "We can't send Grace and Duck in alone."

I nuzzle my nose against Daisy's soft hair while everyone talks around me about how there's no way in hell we're doing what this sick fuck says. I inhale her baby scent and let it infuse my senses. I let it fuel the burning embers of rage simmering beneath my skin. I use her scent to give me the courage to do what fucking needs done.

"I'll do it."

Duck swings his head toward me. "No fucking way."

"I'll do it," I repeat.

"Grace, if you think we're going to let this son of a bitch anywhere near you," Snow begins. "Think fucking again."

I slowly rise to my feet, keeping Daisy protectively against me, as I shift my gaze to each man in the room before letting it land on Snow.

"With all due respect, if you think I'm going to sit back and watch this man, this *Dracula*, play cat and mouse with my family, think. Fucking. Again." Snow's eyes widen at the deadly calm of my words. I shift my eyes to Duck. "And if you think you get the last word when it comes to doing what it takes to protect my family, *our* goddamn family, think. Fucking. Again. I may not be a big, strong biker man with the instincts and drive to kill. But I have one thing not a single one of you can hold a candle to." I kiss the top of Daisy's head. "I have the power and fortitude of a mama bear who will stop at nothing, *not a mother fucking thing*, to make sure danger doesn't get near her cub."

With that, I very quietly leave the room. It doesn't matter to me one iota what else is said in there because at the end of the day, they know I'm not backing down. I'd rather have Duck at my side, but I'll do whatever I have to, with or without him.

CHAPTER 26

DUCK

No one says a word as Grace walks out of the room. Hell, I don't know whether to be shocked, horrified, scared, or all three. One thing I do know is my cock is at attention... again. Damn her and her anger.

Snow clears his throat. "D, I expect you to have a serious conversation with her later about disrespecting the rules in this room." Then his lips start to twitch. "But off the record, lock her down, bro. Any woman who has that big a set of brass balls should be wearing a Satan's Legacy property patch."

I relax at his words. "I plan on it, Prez."

"Good. Now, I'm inclined to let Grace do this."

"Not happening, man," I snap. "I will not put her in danger like that."

"You heard her, D," he counters. "Do you really think us telling her no is gonna stop her?"

Fuck, he's right. She's hell bent on this.

"If I agree, I need to know that I can count on every man in this room."

"I'm gonna chalk it up to all the blood in your head rushing to your cock and pretend you didn't just say that," Carnie snaps from his end of the table. "We all took the same vow of loyalty you did. If you seriously doubt your brothers then I suggest you walk."

"No one's walking anywhere," Snow says. "And Carnie, he still outranks you so keep the disrespect to yourself. I hear it again and you'll have a hefty fine."

"Carnie, man, I didn't mean that I don't trust you. I do. With my life. But just like that fuck had a condition, I've got a few and I need to have all of you on board before I agree to this clusterfuck."

"What are your conditions?"

"Number one: I want our Portland Chapter to send a few brothers to stay here on the compound while the rest of us are out dealing with Dracula. Other than those of us who are on this mission, every single person will go underground and there will be no less than two men at each entrance. One prospect and one patched."

"All in favor of condition one?" Snow asks.

'Ayes' have it.

"Number two: Grace and I will do what he says. We'll go alone to talk to him. But Dip, I need you to scope out the scene ahead of time, find out where you all can be so you can watch over us. Out of sight, but not too far."

"All those in favor?"

'Ayes' again.

"Number three: We are not striking a deal with this prick. Grace and I will play the part, hear him out, but then he's dead."

"All those in favor?"

Everyone agrees.

"And last but not least, number four: If something goes wrong, I want Grace to raise Daisy. She will make sure Daisy knows where she comes from, who her father is, and she will never stay out of touch. I'd love it if they stayed here, on the compound, but that has to be Grace's decision. But, if something happens to both of us..." I pause, my eyes becoming glassy. Even thinking this shit guts me. I take a deep breath before continuing. "If something happens to both Grace and me, Daisy will be raised here, with all of you. Snow, you and Sami will have sole legal custody. She will be your daughter in every way that matters. And if either of these things comes to fruition, none of you let Heather near my little girl. I swear to fucking Christ if you do, I'll climb outta hell and drag you back down into the underworld by your balls."

"Duck, nothing is going to ha—"

I pound the table with a fist. "That's my last condition," I roar. "I don't give a shit if you vote 'aye' or 'nay'. But the only way I'll agree to take this risk is if all four conditions are agreed upon. I have more to think about than just myself now."

"All those in favor?" Snow asks quietly.

One by one, my brothers say 'aye'.

"Snow is there anything else?" I ask him. I need to get the fuck out of this room.

"Actually, I've got something," Spark says.

"Go ahead," Snow urges him.

"I've been working hard to track down a lot of fucking information over the last few months and one of my searches finally paid off."

"How so?" Magic asks.

"Well, remember Phil?"

"Vividly," I snarl. "What about him?"

"I finally had a breakthrough in tracing the number that coordinates were texted from."

"And you couldn't have mentioned this at the beginning of the meeting?" Snow booms.

"Yes, I could have, but you seemed eager to get to the letter."

"Jesus Christ," Snow mumbles. "I'm fining you a hundred bucks just for being stupid. Pay yourself."

Spark takes a hundred dollar bill out of his wallet and shoves it in the envelope he brings to every meeting. Being the treasurer, he collects all fines and he's always prepared.

"Continue."

"Anyway, I have a name."

"Seriously? Two hundred dollars more," Snow barks.

Spark complies, but I can see that his wallet is now empty, so I really hope he doesn't dig himself a deeper hole.

"Devon Chambers. Once I had his name, I was able to search for other phone numbers he might have, bank records, the works. I've been able to tie him to several numbers that link to street level distributors. But here's where it gets tricky. I don't think this guy is Dracula."

"Why?"

"Because once I had a name, any and all information I wanted was easily located. He lives in a condo on the outskirts of Denver. No criminal history. College degree in chemistry but bounces from job to job. He's a nobody."

"Okay. Anything else."

"Yeah. I was only able to link him up with texts that came through. Not actual phone calls. Which tells me that someone else is making the calls with an altered voice. I'm guessing this Devon character is a fall guy."

"So if we agree to this meet with Dracula, we don't

know if we're getting Devon or someone else. Is that what you're saying?"

"Yeah, that's exactly what I'm saying," Spark confirms.

"Well isn't that just fucking great," I gripe.

"Look on the bright side," Snow says. "When you listed your conditions and said you'd do this, we didn't have any name at all. At least now we can be prepared for one scenario."

"Pretty fucking bleak bright side, Prez."

"Spark, can you send us all the information you have on Devon Chambers? That way we know one person we're dealing with."

"On it."

"As for the rest of you, I'll be sending the email to Dracula tomorrow morning, as the letter was post marked two days ago, and as soon as I have the details about the meet, I'll let you know. For now, go drink, go fuck, go home. I don't give a shit which, just get the fuck out of here."

I remain behind with Snow while the rest of them file out.

"What's up, D?"

"I don't like this, Zeke. Not even a little bit."

"I'm not all that crazy about it either, but what choice do we have?"

"I know." I rub my fist into my chest. "Fuck, Zeke, did you see my woman today? She was incredible. And I know I should be upset, but I gotta be honest, all I feel is proud."

"Nothing quite like a mama bear protecting her young."

"That's just it. Daisy isn't hers, not by blood anyway. Grace simply loves her that much. So much that the blood doesn't fucking matter."

"You're preachin' to the choir, D. Remember, I saw how Sami protected Lennox. And Lennox isn't my blood, but it doesn't matter. Blood don't make a family. Satan's Legacy is proof of that."

"How did the two of us get so lucky?"

"I don't know, but I ain't looking to question it too hard."

"No kidding."

"Get outta here, D. Go be with your girls."

I'm out the door in seconds, with Snow's laughter chasing me down the hall.

CHAPTER 27
GRACE

"Remind me again why I agreed to this?"

Duck helps me onto the back of his Harley. Once I'm settled behind him, he wraps a hand around my thigh.

"Because you're stubborn," he says, earning him a slap on the shoulder. "Fine, because you're a mama bear who will stop at nothing to make sure her family is safe."

"Right. Good. Just needed to hear it."

"Are you scared?"

"Aren't you?" I counter.

"Not for me, no. You have to remember, I live and breathe this shit. But for you, for Daisy, yeah, I'm a little scared."

"But everyone will be in place, right? That's what you said."

"Every person on the compound is locked up tight underground. And all the members who will be watching us are already where they're supposed to be."

"Okay then. Let's go."

Duck fires up the Harley. The vibrations calm my racing

heart. Either that, or they mask it. It isn't more than a minute before he takes off down the road toward the gates of the compound. As we crest the hill, I tap him on the shoulder.

Duck brings the bike to a stop and twists to look at me.

"Everything okay?"

"I love you," I blurt. When his eyes widen, I feel the urge to explain. "I do, Duck. I love you. You and Daisy. And I can't go through with this today without you knowing. I need you to know, Duck. I need you to know and believe that I love you with my whole heart."

Duck lowers the kickstand and gets off the bike. He takes my face in his hands and kisses me. I pour my soul into the kiss, wanting him to feel everything I have to give him. He owns me, heart, body, and soul.

When he breaks the kiss, he leans close to my ear and whispers, "I love you, too. So goddamned much. You are the light to my dark. Never, *ever* doubt that. I fucking love you, Grace."

Before either of us can second guess what we're about to do, Duck gets back on the Harley and gets us out of the compound. The location Dracula gave us is an hour outside of the city, so I have plenty of time to think.

Duck made sure I was familiar with every detail regarding Devon Chambers. We still don't know if he's who will be at the abandoned warehouse, but if he is, I'm ready.

Duck also made sure I knew how to shoot a gun, although I hope I don't have to use it. I know that whoever the hell we meet will be killed tonight, but Duck and the guys told me they would do everything in their power to make sure I'm not the one who has to pull the trigger.

And on the off chance that I don't make it out of the warehouse, I'm ready for that too. Don't get me wrong, I don't *want* to die, especially not now that I've had a taste of the family I never thought I would get. But better me than Duck. Daisy needs her father, and I will jump in front of a bullet if it means they can stay together.

Because that's what love is. It's not having babies just because you can or marrying people based on what they can do for you. It's not about who's willing to die for who. And it's definitely not about pain and heartache.

Love is about finding that one person who meets your demons and chooses to fight them alongside you regardless of how much fire they're met with. It's about being content in the knowledge that you would do anything for them, but not telling them because you know they would do the same and you can't bear the thought of them getting hurt. It's about sacrifice and commitment and loyalty. It's about family and friends and memories.

Duck and me... that's love. Duck, Daisy, and me... that's love.

But Duck and Daisy, without me? That is also love.

Which is why I'm content knowing that I'll do anything today to make sure that love can continue to grow. And I didn't tell Duck.

A tap on my leg gets my attention. Duck points ahead of us and I can see the warehouse. We're close. This is it. Sink or swim. Do or die.

Please don't fucking die.

There's already a vehicle in the parking lot. A shiny black Range Rover that I see is empty when Duck pulls up beside it. Duck helps me off the bike, but neither of us says a word. He guides me to the door, and it's unlocked, just like Dracula said it would be.

Duck goes in first, but steps to the side so we can walk together. When the door slams shut behind us, I jump.

"You okay?"

"Peachy."

"We're covered, Grace," he whispers. "We're both walking out of here, okay?"

"I know."

The short hallway spills out into a large, cavernous space. Small windows line the top of each wall, but they're so dirty that not much light spills in. At one time, I'm sure they made the workday a little easier, providing a glimpse of the outside while workers were stuck inside. But today, all they do is make me wonder if our guys can see through them to keep us safe.

Three steps past the hallway and Duck grips my wrist to stop me. He nods forward and I follow his gaze.

Sitting in a chair, with his head hanging low against his chest is a man. We slowly walk toward him, Duck with practiced ease and me with trepidation. Duck lifts the man's head and exposes a single bullet hole between his eyes.

"Well, I guess it's safe to say that Devon isn't Dracula."

"Unless he set this all up only to kill himself, which we both know he didn't. Whoever Dracula is wouldn't be able to take their own life. They'd have to see this through to the end."

"Agreed," Duck says. "So, then, who is Dracula?"

"That's the million dollar—"

A loud bang from the hallway we just walked through has us both spinning around. A very beautiful woman walks toward us, her spike heels clicking on the concrete floor with each step. Duck reaches for my hand and squeezes it. I lift my eyes to his face and see him mouth the words 'I'm sorry'.

For a moment, I wonder what he possibly has to be sorry about, but he doesn't keep me guessing.

"Hello, Heather."

My stomach bottoms out. This is Heather? I never got a good look at her at the hospital the night Daisy was born, so it doesn't surprise me that I didn't recognize her right away. But still... Heather?

"Duck, my love, it's so good to see you," she says in a sugary sweet tone.

"Cut the bullshit," Duck snarls. "You never loved me."

Heather takes a deep breath and sighs. "Yeah, okay. You got me there."

"Wait a minute," I say. "You're Dracula?"

Heather doesn't take her eyes off Duck. "Landed yourself a smart one there, didn't ya? I'll expect an invitation to the wedding, seeing how my actions brought you two lovebirds together."

I lunge for her, but Duck wraps his arms around my waist and holds me against his chest.

"Let me go," I warn.

"Grace, stop," he says harshly against my ear. "Please do not antagonize her."

"You should listen to him, Grace," Heather agrees as she closes the distance between us. She pulls a flip phone out of the pocket of her leather jacket and opens it. "Otherwise, I'll be forced to push this little button here." She shoves the phone in my face and points to the send button. "I'm not too keen on going out in a blaze of glory, if you catch my drift, but beggars can't be choosers."

"What do you want?" Duck asks as he moves me to stand beside him.

"I thought I made that perfectly clear in my letter. I want to strike a deal."

"We can talk deals once you answer some questions," I snap.

"Oh, how cute. You're letting her call the shots." Heather tilts her head. "Funny, when you were fucking me, you never gave me the same courtesy."

"Thank God for that."

"Whatever. You weren't even that good."

Seriously? That's the best comeback she's got? Amateur.

"Lucky for you, I'm in a good mood." She points to Devon's corpse. "Killing always puts me in a better mood."

"Your point?"

"My point, dipshit, is I'll entertain your questions." Heather rests her hand on her hip. "Well, I do have a condition."

"Of course you do. What is it?"

"Grace is the only one who can ask me. And for every question she asks, I get to ask her one back."

"Fine."

"Not a chance."

Duck and I speak at the same time. I look at him and silently plead for him to let me do this. I know he wants to protect me, but I'm already in this all the way up to my eyeballs. Might as well keep going.

"Fine," he caves.

"Oh goody." Heather claps her hands together like a schoolgirl, and I can't stop myself from rolling my eyes. "Why don't we go to the office where it's a little cozier?"

"We're staying right here," Duck barks.

"You always were such a party pooper," Heather pouts for a moment, but then it's like a switch flips and she's a completely different person. Her eyes harden, her face turns to stone, and she squares her shoulders. "Ask your question, bitch," she tells me.

It takes me a minute to think of what to ask. There are a million questions floating around in my mind, but I want to make sure I ask the ones that will be of importance to Duck and the club.

"You better hurry, Grace, before my good mood fades," she warns me.

"Were you ever in love with Duck?"

Heather throws her head back and laughs. "That's your question?" I nod and she shrugs. "Okay, I'll play. No, I never loved him."

Sorry Duck.

"Tit for tat," she sing-songs. "Are you in love with him?"

"Yes." I keep my answer brief. No reason to give her more ammo. "Why'd you agree to marry him?"

"Because he was a means to an end. Satan's Legacy was the biggest supplier in the state. I knew I had quality product, and I needed to learn every single inch of my competition." She takes a breath. "Tit for tat. What's my daughter's name?"

"Daisy. Who's Devon to you?"

"We went to high school together. He's the brains behind the pills and a great fall guy in case you figured it out who I was before I was ready." She looks over at his body and shrugs. "It's a shame I had to kill him. I considered him a friend. Tit for tat. Does Daisy look like me?"

"No. She's every inch her father. Do you really enjoy killing people with your pills?

"Clearly you've never taken a life. Well, other than your daughter of course." Duck growls beside me, but calms when I place my hand on his bicep. "Yes, keep him in line. Anyway, to answer your question, yes, I do. It's powerful, knowing I hold the key to end a person's life. It's a drug of a different kind. Tit for tat. If Duck dies, would you let me see Daisy?"

"Not a fucking chance."

Heather and I go round and round with questions. I lose track of how many are asked. Mine are all geared toward gaining as much knowledge for the club that I can and hers all revolve around Daisy. It's quite pitiful really, watching her act like she gives a shit about the human life she helped create.

"Enough!" Duck shouts, effectively cutting off her little game. "I have one question, Heather, and then we'll talk deals."

"I was wondering how long you'd let her twenty questions bullshit go. I gotta hand it to ya, it was longer than I thought. But it was kinda fun, so go ahead. Ask me one question."

"Was there ever a time that you actually wanted our daughter?"

Heather glances at me and rolls her eyes. "He really doesn't read subtext well, does he? No, Duck. There wasn't. I was on the pill, remember. And then I got sick, and Carnie gave me some antibiotics. What the twisted fuck didn't do is tell me that they may cause my birth control to be ineffective. Now that I think about it, I should have insisted he be here with you both. Afterall, it's his fuck up that forced me to alter my plans."

"Wow. I can't even begin to tell you how grateful I am that you walked away."

"Yes, well, you can thank me later." Heather winks at him. "For old time's sake."

Now, I've been standing here, calmly chatting with evil incarnate, and listening to her glib comments about the man and child I love. And I think I've handled it all with grace, no pun intended. I expected all of her vitriol up to this point. But hearing her proposition Duck snaps my restraint.

In this moment, I can go left, or I can go right. Going right allows Duck to finish this, while going left catapults me forward on a path that will alter who I am for the rest of my life. Spoiler alert, there is never a second of my life, all the way up until I draw my last breath, that I fucking regret going left.

Heather's head whips to the side when my fist connects with her cheek, and she teeters on her impossibly high heels before falling to the floor. She lifts her hand with the flip phone in it, but Duck kicks it away. And then, bless him, he steps back.

For a second, I'm stunned. I didn't think it would be this easy, but then I remind myself it's not over. I step on Heather's chest, forcing her back down when she tries to sit up.

"Not so fast," I sneer.

I grab the gun Duck made me carry in my waistband and flick off the safety. Then I point it at her head.

"What was the deal you wanted to make?" I ask her. It doesn't matter, but she need not know that.

"Why? You interested in climbing into bed with me?"

"I don't know," I lie. "You seem to be doing pretty well for yourself. Maybe I want a cut of the money. Sure would go a long way in raising Daisy."

Heather glances at Duck and tsks. "I like her, Duck. Even with the whole pointing a gun at my head thing." When she looks at me again, she smiles. "My deal, that's what you want to know?"

"Yes."

"Well, I was going to suggest we form an alliance. I'll

continue with production and distribution in Denver. Satan's Legacy would use their contacts through the US to widen distribution. With all the chapters they have, we'd make bank. But I'm not real sure how you would handle distribution all by your lonesome."

"Don't write me off just yet," I tell her. "I'm a nurse, remember? And before I was in Denver, I was a traveling nurse. Think of how many people we could reach using hospitals, how many addicts come to the ER. That's a shit load more people than Satan's Legacy could reach. Even better is that I'd never been in one place for long so it would be near impossible for the cops to catch on."

Heather smiles wide. "I like the way you think. So, do we have a deal?"

She really is as stupid as she looks.

"No. Deal."

I squeeze the trigger, giving her an identical bullet hole to the one she gave Devon.

EPILOGUE

DUCK

One year later...

"**M**ama."

I pull the stroller closer to me and lift Daisy out of it. She struggles to get out of my arms, as she always does. My little girl does not like to sit still. Setting her on her feet, I hold her hands to help her walk toward Grace.

Daisy and I had stayed behind on the bench to give Grace a few minutes alone with her daughter. We make a point to come to the cemetery every few months, something that seems to be helping Grace finally process her grief.

I still remember the first time we came, when I learned her daughter's name for the first time.

"Baby girl, I'd like you to meet some people." Grace talks to *the headstone like she talks to me. "This is Duck. You'd love him.*

And this sweet little thing is Daisy." Daisy babbles and we both chuckle. "Duck, Daisy, this is my daughter, Lynn."

I stare at the headstone and read the name. I don't know how I missed it, but hearing the name out loud finally makes it click.

"Lynn?"

"Yeah. I always liked the name."

"I know. You told me that when I was struggling to come up with a middle name for Daisy," I remind her.

"I know. I'm sorry if it bothers you."

"Bothers me? Baby, it doesn't bother me at all. I'm honored, and I know Daisy will be too when she's old enough to understand."

That day feels like a lifetime ago. I officially made Grace my ol' lady six months ago. We would've tied the knot sooner, but we both agreed to wait until after the Dracula investigation was over.

Turns out, the cops found a warehouse full of red pills and two dead bodies. There was also a note claiming credit to everything Dracula. The cops got their bust, and we got our territory back.

It wasn't even hard to set it all up before calling in an anonymous tip. Heather may have stayed under Satan's Legacy radar for longer than any of us care to admit, but once we had access to her vehicle and GPS history, it wasn't difficult to find her stash and move it.

And I'm thrilled to say, the overdose rates have dropped considerably.

The party at the clubhouse to celebrate was epic and came with a surprise no one was expecting. Toga and Fallon announced that she was pregnant. He never did tell anyone else about the miscarriage. They waited to make the announcement until she was past the first trimester and just as we were heading out of town yesterday to make the drive here, Fallon's water broke. I even received a text this morning with a picture of a little girl and the caption that read 'Welcome baby Callie'.

"Mama, Mama."

Daisy points at Grace, who hears her and begins to rise from her position on the grass.

"Look at you, baby girl. You'll be walking on your own in no time."

"Bite your tongue," I tease. "It's hard enough to keep up with her as it is."

"Oh, Duck, wait until she's a teenager."

"I don't see what'll be so bad about her teenage years. She'll be wearing a chastity belt and confined to the house at all times."

"Duck, I think that would be considered child abuse."

"Fine. But she's already been warned she's not allowed to date until she's thirty."

"Seriously? When did you tell her that?"

"I didn't. Snow did, right after she came home from the hospital."

Grace sweeps Daisy into her arms. "Baby girl, if your daddy or uncles give you any trouble, you come straight to me."

"Mama."

"That's right, Daisy. I'm your mama."

And she is. The adoption papers were finalized within a week of our wedding. As the saying goes, everyone has a price. The judge that rushed the finalization for us, really likes his heroin, but not the publicity that goes along with getting caught with it. He fucks up, he calls us, and we take care of it. At least for the next three years. After that, he's on his own.

"You about ready to go?" I ask her and tip my head back. "Looks like it's gonna rain, and I hate driving on slick roads with you and Daisy in the car."

Yes, I'm that dad. Get over it.

"Almost. I just need a few more minutes."

"Okay, I'll take Daisy and we'll wait on the bench for you."

Grace shakes her head. "No, stay. Please."

I nod. Grace takes a hold of my hand and pulls me closer. "Lynn, sweetheart, Mommy has to go. But first, I have something I want to tell you. You're gonna be a big sister again."

"What did you just say?"

Grace shifts my hand to her stomach, just below where Daisy is resting on her side.

"I'm pregnant."

"You're... really?"

"Yeah." Grace turns around. "Reach into my back pocket."

I do as she says and pull out a grainy black and white photo. I recognize it immediately as an ultrasound image.

"That's... Shit..." I stutter. "That's our baby."

"That's our baby."

"We're gonna have a baby."

"We're gonna have a baby," she repeats.

"Baby," Daisy mimics.

I lift Daisy out of Grace's arms and swing her around. She giggles and the sound is music to my ears. "Yeah, Daisy, baby."

Grace faces the headstone again, and I catch sight of a tear sliding down her cheek. "It's really time, Lynn." She kisses her fingers and presses them against the granite. "I love you."

The three of us leave the cemetery, and it's bittersweet, as it always is. I know Grace hates walking away from her first born, but she loves coming home. And really, Lynn will always be wherever Grace is.

Once we're back in the hotel and Daisy is asleep for the night in her portable crib, Grace and I shower and then climb naked under the covers on the king-size bed. I pull her toward me, her back to my front, and rest my hand over her belly.

A lot has happened since Grace and I met. Some of it was bad, although most of it was good. But I've had a question burning a hole in my brain since that day in the warehouse with Heather. And now that we're bringing another life into this world, I don't want there to be any lingering questions.

"What has you thinking so hard, Duck?"

I smile into her hair. "How'd you know?"

"I can feel it. You're always a little more tense when you're deep in thought."

"I love you."

"I love you, too. Now quit stalling. What's on your mind?"

I take a deep breath. "Back in that warehouse, with Heather..."

"Go on," she prods gently when I get quiet.

"Why didn't you let me end it? Why did you kill her? You know I didn't want that for you."

Grace flips over so she's facing me and cups my jaw. "I was wondering when you'd ask me that."

"You were?"

"Yeah. I always knew the day would come when you simply had to know. I guess today is the day."

"Today is the day," I confirm.

"Before I answer you, I need you to know that I don't regret putting a bullet between that woman's eyes. I don't regret it, I don't lose sleep over it, and I would do it again a thousand times."

"Okay."

"The simple answer is I did it because I love you."

"And the not so simple answer?"

"I did it so you wouldn't have to. I never wanted there to come a day when you had to tell Daisy that you killed her biological mother. Because make no mistake Duck, there *will* come a day when Daisy has questions. That is a burden no father should have to carry. I did it so I could carry the burden for you."

And that is reason number eight million and one why I love my ol' lady.

Next in the Satan's Legacy MC Series

Dip's Flame

Dip...

I'm not a good man, and I've never pretended otherwise. As the Road Captain of Satan's Legacy MC, I've seen and done things most wouldn't be proud of, but me? I couldn't care less. Good, bad, or indifferent, I am who I am, and you either accept me or don't.

That has always been the way I lived my life. Until the night I walk into a bar and see her. She shouldn't captivate me the way she does, but those eyes, those tits, and that mouthwatering ass suck me in. Despite that, it's clear she doesn't belong here. She's a good girl, a nice girl, a girl I could corrupt in a heartbeat.

So when she gives me a proposition, how can I say no?

Kennedy...

When I got married at nineteen, it was because I had to. My husband was chosen for me by the church, and I had no say in any of it.

But now I'm a widow, and my life is just beginning. For the first time in ten years, I feel in control, and all I want to do is lose it, throw caution to the wind and experience all the sins I can without damning myself to Hell.

And I think I know just the person to help me do it.

About the Author

Andi Rhodes is an author whose passion is creating romance from chaos in all her books! She writes MC (motorcycle club) romance with a generous helping of suspense and doesn't shy away from the more difficult topics. Her books can be triggering for some so consider yourself warned. Andi also ensures each book ends with the couple getting their HEA! Most importantly, Andi is living her real life HEA with her husband and their boxers.

Also by Andi Rhodes

Broken Rebel Brotherhood

Broken Souls

Broken Innocence

Broken Boundaries

Broken Rebel Brotherhood: Complete Series Box set

Broken Rebel Brotherhood: Next Generation

Broken Hearts

Broken Wings

Broken Mind

Bastards and Badges

Stark Revenge

Slade's Fall

Jett's Guard

Soulless Kings MC

Fender

Joker

Piston

Greaser

Riker

Trainwreck

Squirrel

Gibson

Satan's Legacy MC

Snow's Angel

Toga's Demons

Magic's Torment

Duck's Salvation

Dip's Flame

Devil's Handmaidens MC

Harlow's Gamble

Printed in Great Britain
by Amazon